GET **MORE** GROUP CLIENTS

The Objection Free Approach to Selling More Business
Than You Ever Thought Possible

BY MEL SCHLESINGER

ISBN: 145372303X
ISBN-13: 9781453723036

INTRODUCTION

GET MORE GROUP CLIENTS

Welcome to this introductory lesson to The **Get More Group Clients System**. The goal of this introduction to give you an idea of what this system is about. This book was designed to be a 10 week course but you may choose to complete it in less time or you may choose to work this out over a number of months. What I can tell you with absolute certainty is this: the techniques taught in this course have helped many of my clients significantly increase their revenue. One of my clients, Tom Avery went from $4000 monthly to over $30,000 monthly in less than two years. To be fair, he was already doing many things well such as having a lot of appointments. Tom simply needed to learn how to improve the quality of those appointments and how to engage the prospect in a different kind of a conversation. Another client – Howard Silverstein, used one simple technique that I refer to as the "Strong Opening Statement" and generated a case worth $14,000 in annual commission.

Feel free to email me with any questions or thoughts. So now let us begin!

Sales Person or Consultant?

Ask any Employee Benefit Professional whether he considers himself a salesperson or a consultant and 100% of the time the answer is the latter. This idea of being a consultant is so pervasive that most benefit professionals will actually take offense if you even hint that they are really salespeople. Somewhere along the line the idea of being a salesperson became inconsistent with the image of being a professional. If you ask anyone to describe a salesperson to you, words like manipulative, high-pressure, self-serving and unprofessional will be top of the list. But where did this notion of the salesperson being less professional than a consultant come from? For any avid reader of books on the art and science of selling the answer is obvious. Most books (and trainers for that matter) focus on skills like closing and objection handling. Any salesperson that has been around for any length of time knows about "trial closes" and at least two methods for dealing with objections.

Companies spend thousands of dollars every year on one and two-day sales training programs in an attempt to teach their team methodologies that will make them more effective salespeople. And the great majority of these programs focus on the consultative approach to selling, an approach that appeals to the desire to be anything but a salesperson. These sales methodologies are overly complex and as most organizations will readily admit, 30 days post-training the sales team is doing what they have always done. More than anything else, it is the complexity of the methodologies that make them so prone to being ignored. Fortunately, the art of selling is not really all that complex. The complexity is born out of a certain necessity that is created by publishers who expect a minimum number of pages before a book can be published and the desire of in-house training departments to make choices based not so much on the effectiveness of the methodology but on the complexity of the program. Training departments tend to believe that the more complex the program the more likely that it is the better option.

Two years ago I traveled to Connecticut to meet with the Vice President of Sales for a large health insurance company. This company had just concluded a multi-year contract with a major sales training company and was less than enthusiastic with the results. They were now late in the process of looking for a new training organization to work with their representatives. It is important to understand that the sales representatives of this carrier did not sell to the end user but rather called on Employee Benefit Professionals in an attempt to get them to place business with the carrier. Calling on the Benefit Professional requires a somewhat different skill set than calling on the end-user. I happen to have an expertise in this area since I had built a successful General Agency by working with the same target audience that the carrier's representatives were calling on. As I chatted with the training department team it became obvious that they were going to choose another national training company. The leader of the team even went and retrieved the various forms that my competitor was going to use during training. In looking at these forms it was obvious that they were designed to aid in the sale to the end-user as opposed to a third-party referrer. The V.P. acknowledged that these forms were directed at the end-user but felt strongly that the half-day that would be spent on using them would yield some value. The end result is that this carrier went from one national training company with a complex sales strategy to another with an even more complex sales strategy and the results have been no better. In fact when I meet representatives of this carrier and ask about the training they simply laugh.

Before we go any further let me share my view of the distinction between salesperson and consultant. The benefit consultant is an individual that is hired by a company and **_paid a fee_** for his assistance in developing a strategy to help achieve a corporate objective. The benefit salesperson represents a carrier or carriers and is **_paid a commission_** for the sale of their product or products. The distinction of fee versus commission is a very important distinction but it does not imply that one is better than the other. This particular distinction has never been as important as it is in today's benefit marketplace. As health insurance companies have reduced commissions most insurance agents have complained about the impact on their businesses and their ability to earn a living. While everyone pays lip-service to the ideal that "I do not care about commissions. I only care about what is best for the client," the world of lowered commissions has shown the importance of commissions on how we operate. Agents now tell me that all things being equal they will take into consideration where they are with respect to achieving higher compensation levels due to production when choosing carriers. Still, being on commission does not automatically preclude doing a good job for the client. The question is: how do we sell our services, make a good living without working ourselves to death and still provide meaningful service to the consumer? Let us take a look at the different types of salesperson as seen in illustration 1 on the next page.

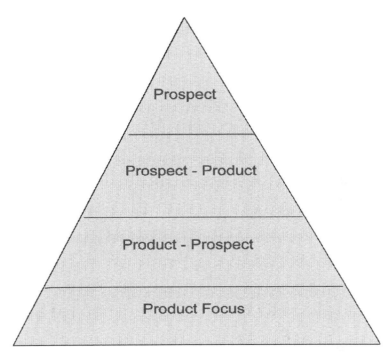

Figure 1 – Sales Pyramid

The Product Focus

At the very bottom of the pyramid we find the salesperson who has one focus and one focus only and that is to make the sale. This was the historic teaching of my sales methodologies. For this salesperson it is all about closing and objection handling and making the sale whether or not the prospect wants or needs the product.

My first encounter with this type of hardcore selling was in 1978 when I was hired to sell in-ground pools and spas in San Diego, California. Prospects would come into the showroom to look at the demo spa and the various models. It was my job to secure an in-home appointment for the purpose of getting measurements for a formal price. The owner had taught me that there might be a Running Back, a Half-Back and a Quarter-Back, but there was no such a thing as a Be-Back. If you did not make the sale while in the home you were done. With that in mind I would get secure a 6:30 PM appointment with the promise that I would be out in 45 minutes. It was not uncommon for me to still be in the home at midnight. The prospect was either going to buy or call the cops! Once in the home it was all about putting on performance. If the prospect said "no" or "I need to think about it" I had several different ways to deal with it – some not so ethical.

Another example closer to home was an experience that I had in 1988 selling an individual health insurance policy through one of the "Self-Employed" associations and not the one most commonly thought of. This particular organization sold a hospital-surgical policy with an optional outpatient benefit rider that paid 80% of expenses up to an annual maximum of $100,000. The company supplied pre-set appointments and the underwriting carrier was A.M. Best A+ rated. Each Friday I would attend the weekly sales meeting where the manager and others would turn in four, five or six applications and I would turn in one or two. My dilemma was that if a prospect had high quality, major medical coverage with Time Insurance or World Insurance, the premium for comparable coverage with our carrier was significantly higher.

When I shared this with the manager, the following conversation transpired:

Manager: Were any of the prospects under the age of 35?

Me: About half of them were. Why?

Manager: You just ask them how often they have gone to the doctor in the last couple of years. When they say "not at all", you ask them if they really want to pay for outpatient coverage for doctors. They will say that they do not want the rider and then our plan is less expensive.

Me: But isn't that unethical?

Manager: You're fired! Get out of here!

This is a prime example of being Product-Focused. So where did this approach to sales begin? Read most of the older books on selling and you read about techniques such as getting the prospect to say yes to small, inconsequential things such as: "Saturday's with the family are great, aren't they?" The idea is to get the prospect comfortable saying yes to you so that when you go for the close getting a "yes" is easy. There are the various trial closes that help the prospect make small decisions about your product or service so that the closing decision is not quite so big a deal. For the most part this product focus is found primarily in the in-home selling situation or any one-on-one selling situation. It is very hard to use this approach in the employee benefit arena.

Product - Person

Salespeople in this category are still focused on the product sale but they operate from the perspective of only selling products that they believe the prospect needs. The operative phrase in this context is "that they believe is needed." Early in my insurance career I knew a life insurance agent named Robert. Robert so believed in life insurance that he would often sell premiums that amazed me. He had a 90% closing ratio and once explained to me that he felt that he owed it to the prospect to sell him as much life insurance as he could. When I asked if he did not feel a little bad for the amount of high pressure that he applied he responded by saying: "Mel, I have never talked to a widow who complained that I had sold her husband too much life insurance." In this case the salesperson believes that he is not simply focused on selling a product but on helping the prospect.

In the world of employee benefits this can often be seen in the world of voluntary benefits. Several years ago I was coaching a sales representative for a carrier known nationally as a leader in the sale of cancer and accident insurance. One day I asked this agent how she would respond if an employer stated that he was interested in offering a cancer policy only. She told me that she would try to explain the benefits of offering the full portfolio of voluntary products. I then asked how she would respond to only being allowed to sell cancer insurance. Amazingly, she said that during the enrollment she would let the employees know that she had other products available and if anyone wanted to buy something she would gladly sell it to them because "they really need the coverage." In this case her client is the employer who explicitly stated his desires but her desire to sell more of her products was more important.

When the salesperson believes that he knows what is best and is focused on selling the product at all costs the person becomes a secondary consideration. Like the product-focused salesperson there will be a need to rely on sales tactics that are manipulative and high-pressure. It is like the cookware salesperson who said: "When a prospect answers the door I know that he has my money in his pocket because I have his cookware in my car!" Need and desire on the part of the prospect is irrelevant.

Person – Product

This level is the beginning of enlightened salesmanship. The idea of using manipulative sales techniques is anathema. The focus here is on doing what is right for the client. Most of the employee benefit salespeople that I talk with are at this level of the Pyramid. Benefit salespeople at this level will say things like: "I never look at commissions because I am only interested in what is best for the client" and "I want my clients to get the best benefits for their money." While this sounds very altruistic it is not always in the best interest of the client, but that is for a later discussion. The point is that at this level of the Pyramid there is a very real concern for the client. That said, this particular salesperson still has a product focus.

The product focus is most obviously seen by the general reluctance to engage in a cross-selling discussion with prospects and clients. For the great majority of benefit salespeople appointments are secured by way of accumulating renewal dates and then quoting on health plans as they receive their rate increases. Salespeople at this level will quote the health insurance but they avoid discussing any benefits not already in place. If the employer currently offers dental and group term life this agent will quote them but will avoid a discussion of short-term disability. If there are voluntary benefits in place the agent may or may not quote them as well. And if there are no voluntary benefits in place this agent will almost definitely not initiate the discussion of them. In fact, as I call on these agents about ancillary products a common response is: "If one of my clients asks me about these products I will call you." This is a real clue that there is still a product focus.

There are a number of common rationales for this attitude.

1. I do not want to seem pushy
2. There is so much to know about what I do that I cannot possibly be good at selling these other products
3. You can only really be good at one thing and mine is health insurance
4. I am an advisor and if my clients have an interest they will call me

The problem is that these are simply excuses that hide the fact that this is about fear of selling. One of my first coaching clients engaged my services because he wanted to grow his income stream but like most successful group health agents had found that he was so busy with renewals and service work that there was little time for new prospecting. We developed a cross-selling strategy focused on executive carve-out disability income. The first client that he approached had been with him for more than six years so he felt confident that he could open a new opportunity. Much to his chagrin he discovered that they had implemented a plan two years earlier through another agent. When he inquired about their reasons for not calling him first they replied that they did not know that he did executive carve-out disability income coverage. They thought that he only sold group health insurance. If your clients think that you only sell group health you cannot argue that you do not have a product focus at some level.

Another clue that this agent is at the Person – Product level is the inclusion of the spreadsheet in the benefit proposal. One of my favorite questions for the benefit professional to ask a prospect is this: "When I return would you like me to provide a spreadsheet of all of the plans that I receive quotes on or just the one or two that I think a best suited to your goals?" One hundred percent of the time the reply is: "I just want to know what you think I should do." Prospects would prefer not to have to look at the spreadsheet because it only confuses the issues for them. Even if you tell them which plan you believe is best for their goals they will still feel the need to review that spreadsheet which leads to those six hated words: "I want to think about it!" Not long ago I was coaching with an agency in California where the goal was to shorten the sales cycle, increase closing ratios and get more referrals. The agency president was very resistant to the idea of eliminating the spreadsheet. His reasoning was that his prospects expected it. To my inquiry about whether they wanted it he replied "absolutely." But when I asked how he knew that prospects wanted a spreadsheet he could not answer. To my suggestion that on his next appointment he actually ask the prospect he replied that he could not do that. His reasoning was that if he did not include a spreadsheet which proved that he actually received quotes from all of the available carriers he might lose a case to a competitor that shows something that he hadn't. This attitude is much more about the agent's interests than it is about the prospect's interests. This is not the focus of the consultant but of someone still focused on making a sale rather than developing a strategy designed to help the client achieve his goals.

The Person Focus

At the pinnacle we have the benefit professional that is completely focused on the prospect's goals and objectives rather than a specific product. The appointment may be about the group health plan but this professional understands that you cannot shop the health plan without understanding the prospect's overall benefit objectives. While many salespeople think that this is the level that have attained the truth is that this is a very difficult position to fill. At this level we are engaging in creative thinking about benefit planning. Figure 1-2 illustrates the way the Benefit Professional should look at the world of employee benefits.

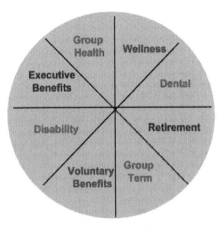

The Complete Benefit Professional

Figure 1-2: The World of Benefits

As can be seen from the above illustration the world of employee benefits is about much more than just group health insurance. The products in red represent the most commonly discussed benefits by the group producer. The purple represents products that some benefit salespeople will include and they are natural fit for the benefit planning. The blue represent areas that are generally ignored by most employee benefit salespeople. But at the top of the pyramid the benefit professional will ask the type of questions that uncover an employer's goals that can be fulfilled by including these products and services. The Benefit Professional at this level of the pyramid is no longer salesperson but a true partner in co-creating the benefit plans design for the client.

The Benefit Professional with a real focus on the client understands that the client does not want a spreadsheet of options but wants a solution to his dilemma. A spreadsheet is not a solution. Presenting a solution entails risk on the part of the benefit professional. But if the client can see how the solution will help him achieve his goals it is unlikely that a competitor will win the case. A solution does not contain a list of every potential service that the benefit professional can deliver but it does include those services that will help in achieving the client's goals. If the prospect did not explicitly state that COBRA administration was important then COBRA is not included in solution. At this level it is not about overwhelming them with a list of services but it is about creating the "Wow" factor by accurately selecting services that contribute to their explicitly state objectives.

You will know that you are the top of the pyramid when after a presentation a prospect says that no one has asked the type of questions that you did. Another clue is if the prospect has talked more than 75% of the time that you met. If you are doing most of the talking you are very likely at the Person-Product level of the Pyramid. The goal of the book is to get you to the top of the Sales Pyramid. Once at the top you will convert more prospects into clients, get more Agent of Record Letters and make more money with less effort. At the top of the Pyramid you become completely client-centered and give up any focus on a specific product.

The goal of the 10 Weeks to Objection-Free Selling course is to get you to the top of the pyramid where you are 100% focused on helping the prospect identify what he really wants to accomplish even though he not even know what that is. Then choosing your products based on the prospect's desired outcomes.

At the end of this program you will have a steady flow of new high quality prospects who want to meet with you. You will be able to get those prospects to tell you exactly what you need to do to close the sale. Finally you will deliver a proposal that is explicitly linked to the prospects stated goals.

With that I wish you good luck and good selling.

LESSON 1

FEATURES BENEFITS AND ADVANTAGES

As I discussed previously, most employee benefit professionals do not actually view themselves as salespeople. Several years ago I was engaged by a Denver Colorado employee benefit agency to provide a one-day sales training program. During lunch I asked one of the salespeople how she felt about the morning's program and to my dismay she replied: "I thought that it was interesting but I hate the idea of selling." Since the entire morning was focused on how to identify the goals of an employer, I was a bit perplexed so I asked her why she was so opposed to selling. She explained that she would never sell a product that wasn't needed and more importantly she would never use any manipulative techniques to make someone buy a product. Personally, I did not think that the techniques that I taught were manipulative.

It is critically important to understand that professional selling has absolutely nothing to do with manipulation or making someone buy something that they neither need nor want. For our purposes let's define selling as: "The ability to engage a prospect in a Compelling Conversation with the goal of helping achieve his goals." This can only be accomplished by a sales professional who is at the top of the Sales Pyramid. As a professional salesperson your goal is not to create a need, convince someone that you have the best product, or make someone buy an unnecessary product. The best salesperson is really the best consultant.

Before we move on I want to make clear that I believe that being a great salesperson is the single most important job in this country. There is no doubt that you probably think that I have lost my mind, but bear with me. The first thing to recognize that nothing can happen at all until you sell something. All of the people at the various carriers that you represent only have jobs because you sell their products. The underwriters, the policy issue folks, the customer service representatives and the carrier reps all have jobs that depend on you. Periodically I get asked about teachers, doctors, fire response, police and clergy as perhaps having a more important role in this country's wellbeing. But the truth is that the professional salesperson is the reason that we have all of those specialties. The teacher owes his job to the salesperson. Because of the sales that he makes there are many people who earn salaries on which taxes are paid. It is these taxes that pay the salaries of the teachers, police and fire fighters. Even the doctor owes the ability of his patients to pay for his services to the salespeople that help keep these patients employed. And as benefit salesperson, it is your job to insure that they have the health insurance to pay for the healthcare they receive.

I engaged in the last section because it is important to know that being a salesperson is a more noble profession than being a consultant. The entire world runs simply because you sell products to people who can benefit from them. It is not about calling on a prospect and knowing that he has your money in his checking account because you have his health insurance application in your briefcase (a little liberty with a Zig Ziglar quote). The professional salesperson helps the consumer verbalize his goals in way that allows you to help him achieve them.

The Root of All Objections

Hopefully you are now excited about the idea of being a professional salesperson and want to take your skills to a new level. Every sales training prospect that has inquired about my services has asked about objection handling skills. Personally I do not believe in objection handling. To me a "no" means no. I hate it when a salesperson does not listen to me when I say no to his proposition. When a prospect says "no" he is not saying that he needs more information. A prospect's "no" means that you did a poor job at establishing how your sales proposition is going to get him something that he wants. In the world of the Compelling Conversation™ our goal is to have an objection-free presentation. There are three mistakes that salespeople make that actually create the objections that they get. The first mistake is an attempt to identify a need or a problem. Mistake number two is providing too much information. The final and most common mistake is launching into a premature presentation.

Mistake # 1 – Needs and Problems

Virtually every sales book that I have ever read talks about identifying a need, a problem of finding the pain. But every group producer can talk about the many cases where the prospect agreed that there was a need or problem and still took no action. Let me ask you this question: have you ever met with a prospect that openly stated that the current broker was not doing a very good job and yet chose to stay with the incumbent anyway? Several months ago, I had a telephone call from an agent in Fayetteville, North Carolina about a case that she had been working on and lost to the incumbent. She told me that on the first appointment the president of the company agreed that the incumbent had not been living up to expectations. As she went through her list of questions she discovered that the company did not have a plan to effectively communicate benefits, they were doing COBRA in-house and were looking to reduce the cost of the health plan. After shopping the plan she identified a Blue Cross Blue Shield of NC plan that would significantly reduce premiums without sacrificing a lot of benefit. She included COBRA administration and employee benefit communications as well as the opportunity to have single source billing. Confident that this was in the bag she asked the president if he would like to move forward and schedule the enrollment. Much to her chagrin he replied that he felt an obligation to ask the incumbent if he could provide these benefits. She assumed that since the president stated his dissatisfaction with the incumbent there was a need to change. She also assumed that since he did not have these other services which were "needed" in her opinion (another error) this was a no-brainer." Unfortunately for her, the president felt that a known was always better than an unknown and he stayed with the incumbent.

The second error is a very common mistake that benefit brokers make. They think that because they believe something has value it must be true. It is important that value is always a personal perspective. One of my coaching clients called me last week to ask about a strategy to obtain an agent of record letter on a twenty-five employee group. Needless to say that I was surprised when he informed me that only seven of the twenty-five were covered on the health plan. Apparently the employer only pays 50% of the employee premium so 18 of the employees felt that the money was better spent elsewhere. To my suggestion that he approach the employer with a strategy to implement a limited medical plan he replied that the employees **needed** a major medical plan. When I asked if they needed a plan that would pay for doctor visits and offset the cost of some other healthcare expenses, he replied that what they needed was real coverage. If you do not take anything else away from reading this book, remember this: people are not motivated by needs. More importantly, what you believe that a prospect needs is irrelevant.

Mistake # 2 – Too Much Information

While providing too much information is a problem with most salespeople, it is a major obstacle to the employee benefit professional. In an attempt to be thorough the benefit professional provides so much information that it becomes impossible for the prospect to make a decision. The over-providing of information can be seen in three distinct areas:

1. Providing too much personal background on the broker and/or the agency
2. Listing every possible service that can be offered as well as every carrier that the broker represents
3. The spreadsheet

The science of behavioral economics teaches us that the more information that an individual has the more time they need they to digest that information. Rather than helping the client make a good decision we complicate the process with information overload. Let's take a brief look at each of these areas of information overload.

Personal Background

If you are like 90% of the benefit professionals that I have spoken with, after your warm-up you open most first appointments with:

"Mr. Prospect, before we talk about your benefits let me tell you a little about my background and my agency. I have been in the benefits business for 100 years and have many very satisfied clients. I represent every major carrier in the area and some that aren't so major, that way I can find you the program that is best for your need. Here is my brochure and as you can see we can provide many important services such as COBRA Administration, Claims management and Section 125 Plans. If you choose to work with us I guarantee that you will get great service. The question that you should answer before going further is: why do you do that? The answers that I generally get are:

- ➢ How else will the prospect know that I have the requisite knowledge?
- ➢ The client needs to know that I will shop every major carrier
- ➢ It helps build trust

I can assure you that the new prospect does not care at all about your background or your agency. The reason for this is that the prospect knows that everything that you say is self-serving and therefore they pay little attention to it. If this was important to them you would never hear: "Let me think about it."

The List of Services

This is generally found both at the initial meeting as well as in the front of the proposal at time of presentation. When used, the rationale is that if the broker doesn't list all of the potential services available and another broker offers one that he failed to show, that could cost him the case. In truth, when you use this approach you may lose the case because of one single service that you failed to show, but that doesn't mean that the service was important. This approach simply converts what you do into a commodity. And commodities are the one instance where size really does matter. Since the list of services has no connection to the actual desires of the prospect they are forced to make a choice by counting the number of services being offered. The longest list wins. Early in my career I lost a payroll deduction cancer case because I used this approach. Rather than focus on specific benefits I wheeled out a list of features and told the Human Resources Manager to compare against the competition. Unfortunately, another carrier had a longer, although less valuable list of features, but alas it was too late to save the case.

The Spreadsheet

There is no bigger mistake that a broker can make than to include the spreadsheet. First – on your next appointment ask the prospect this question: "When I return I can bring you a spreadsheet containing every quote that I get or I can bring you the one or two solutions that I think is best. Which would you prefer?" I guarantee that the prospect will, with a great sigh of relief tell you to just bring the one plan that you think would be best!

The prospect does not want nor does he need to see all of the information. Alok Jha, science correspondent for the Guardian in the Friday, February 17, 2006 issue discussed the problem with too many choices.

"He asked volunteers to pick their favourite car from a list of four based on a set of four attributes including fuel consumption and passenger leg room. He gave them four minutes to think about their decision and most people chose the car with the most plus points. When Dr Dijksterhuis made the experiment more complex - 12 attributes rather than four - people could only identify the best car a quarter of the time. This result was no better than choosing at random."

The four versus twelve attributes is similar to offering a single solution versus the spreadsheet. When you use a spreadsheet, even though you may share your recommendation, the prospect has no choice but to want time to sift through the varied choices on that spreadsheet. Again, if the spreadsheet had value virtually none of your prospects would need to think about the decision.

Unfortunately, two things happen when you include the spreadsheet. The first is information overload. No matter how you may try to simplify the information there will be way too much for the average person to digest. Plus, because of regulatory restraints, you are limited in how much of the carrier's proposal you can eliminate for the sake of simplification. So, you are forced to include a lot of minutiae which makes deciphering the spreadsheet very complicated.   The second problem is that the spreadsheet makes price the focus rather than your value. The spreadsheet gives the prospect a list to compare. If every broker quotes the local Blue Cross plans then it is likely that you all have the same quote. In order to aid in the choice, the prospect simply looks at each spreadsheet and chooses the person with the most options.

It is important to recognize that most of the major brokers in your area all offer a similar menu of services and all of them also sell the same carriers that you do. If you reduce what you do to a list, whether in a spreadsheet or a list of services that will be how you will judged.

Mistake #3 – The Premature Presentation

There are two examples of the Premature Presentation. In the first case the agent arrives for the first meeting and engages in the mistakes above. Before knowing anything about the prospect he launches into a litany of everything that he can do. But it is the second mistake that results in brokers thinking they have a live buyer but end up with no sale. This occurs where the prospect begins to ask questions. If the broker has had any sales training, he thinks that these questions are buying signs, but they are not! A coaching client of mine called me recently to discuss a case that he had been sure he was going to close only to lose it to the incumbent. The reason he was sure that he was going to get this case was that the prospect asked really good questions during his meeting and he believed that that was a buying sign. One of the questions had to do with enrolling the locations in the southern part of the state. In response to the question my client launched into a premature presentation of his state-wide enrollment capability and how he would be able to service these other locations on a regular basis. Unfortunately, he never uncovered why the prospect was asking this question. Another question posed by the prospect was about the number of support staff. Once again my client simply answered the question by not only stating the number of staff but explaining what each of them did in his office as well as an additional service that he contracts with for specific clients.

When you launch into a presentation before you know the specific objectives of the prospect, whether it is in response to a question or to "wow" the prospect you risk creating an objection later. When my client responded to the query on staff with an explanation of people and roles he risked the objection of: "Well, my current broker has more staff and they assign a personal assistant to my HR department." When he launched into a presentation of his statewide enrollment capabilities he inadvertently added fuel to the objection fire. It is possible that during a premature presentation you will hit on something meaningful to the prospect but it is highly unlikely. People only pay attention to what they are really interested in and a question does not convey interest.

Three Questions

So, if identifying needs and problems is the cause of most objections then what is selling all about?

If making sure that the prospect has all of the information necessary to make a meaningful decision causes objections then what do we do, not provide information?

Don't we have to answer a prospect's questions and doesn't that show interest?

Chchchchanges

If I asked you to identify your single biggest competitor, could you? I know that you think you can but you would be so very wrong. You see, at the end of the day there is one thing that your prospect can always choose to do – and that is nothing! You number one competitor is not another agent but the status quo. Every agent reading this book has had the prospect that stated unequivocally that he was less than satisfied with the incumbent and then chose to remain with him. It is not because people are resistant to change, although that is a myth that most people believe, but because you did not do anything that motivated the prospect to change.

People are not by nature averse to change. Change is what we are all about. Ask yourself these questions:

- ✓ Did you start out in insurance or did you begin in another career?
- ✓ Have you ever quit a job to take another?
- ✓ Have you ever traded in a perfectly good car to buy another?
- ✓ Have you earned a credential such as the REBC or the RHU or the CLU?
- ✓ Have you sold a home and purchased a new one?

If you answered any of these questions "yes" then you not only have experienced change but very often you initiated change. In fact if you look at your life you can identify many different times where you willingly initiated change.

When you call on a business owner or human resource professional you are asking them to make a change. The change may be from another broker to you, from one carrier to another, a change in plan design or benefits offered. Ultimately this is about change and motivating the prospect to make it. So if we are not resistant to change the real question that we ought to be asking is: "What motivates someone to willingly embrace some change while resisting other changes with every fiber of their being?"

Voluntary versus Involuntary Change

The first step in understanding change is to recognize that how we perceive the change has a huge impact on how we react. Think back to an experience where you felt like change was being forced on you. Perhaps it was as a child when your parents told you that you had to pick-up your toys. How did you respond to the command that you have to? What about at work? Have you had a situation where you were being told that you had to do something or that you had to do it a certain way? When we are faced with this "have to" approach to change we tend to dig in our heels and refuse to change. I know that as a kid I purposely left my toys on the living room floor just because I was not going to be told what to do.

When you try to focus on needs with a prospect the same result occurs. An employer asks about accident insurance and you believe that that is a waste of money. You know that what the group needs is disability income insurance so you begin to try to educate the employer on why this is true. The employer may even agree that disability income makes more sense but chooses to do nothing or worse, buys an accident plan from a competitor. This actually happened to me early in my career. I almost lost a big dental case over this exact scenario of accident versus disability income.

Voluntary change on the other hand is initiated by the individual. Have you ever been out on a Saturday at the

Mall with no intention of buying anything when you saw something that you really wanted and came home with it? That is an example of a voluntary change. The change was in how you used your money. You had a lot of choices including saving those dollars but chose to change the amount of money in your possession because you wanted something. Understand that need had no role in this decision. In fact we often spend money on things that we want but do not need. And there is the secret to change: find what the prospect wants.

Another example of this can be found in New Year's resolutions such as weight loss or exercise. Ask anyone why they are making this resolution and the reply will be that they need to start exercising or they need to lose weight. It is completely irrelevant whether the change is self initiated or externally initiated, when it is about needs it is doomed to fail. So our goal as benefit professionals is to identify what it is that a prospect wants, what his goals are for his benefit plan. If we can identify what a prospect wants, then we can craft a presentation that is based on how we are going to help him achieve his goals. But that is easier said than done.

I Don't Know What I Don't Know

Despite what most benefit professionals think the great majority of our conversations are extremely superficial. The benefit professional asks questions such as: "What would you like for me to do for you?" and hears: "Keep my premiums down," and then goes to work on that premise. Another common response from a prospect is that they want a strong network or they want a plan that provides a minimal office visit co-pay for their employees. The intrepid benefit professional then gets the current plan design and rates and proceeds to get quotes from various carriers based on this meaningless information. This is not to insult the many benefit professionals reading this book, but it is a fact. You see, when you ask what is important and the prospect says premiums, he doesn't really mean premiums, it is just that he doesn't know how to tell you the real issues.

We all know that employers offer benefits for a variety of reasons such as to attract quality employees, minimize turnover, motivate employees to be more productive, lower pressure for increased wages and many other reasons. Unfortunately, the prospect isn't thinking in those terms. Because most benefit professionals simply take these superficial answers and shop the health plan, the prospect assumes that that is all there is to the benefits business. This is why an employer that is dissatisfied with the incumbent stays with him anyway. It is the job of the complete benefit professional to help the prospect identify what is really important and we do that by asking really good questions. Consider the difference between these two dialogues:

Conversation 1

Agent: Mr. Prospect, in terms of today's meeting, what were you hoping to accomplish?

Prospect: I was hoping that you can tell me how you are going to help me get my health insurance premiums down.

Agent: Well, after I get some information I will shop your health plan with all of the local carriers and try to identify the most cost effective way for you to still provide meaningful benefits and still reduce your cost.

Prospect: Do you have any ideas?

Agent: Absolutely! Have you considered an HSA plans design?

Conversation 2

Agent: Mr. Prospect, in terms of today's meeting, what were you hoping accomplish.

Prospect: I was hoping that you can tell me how you are going to help me get my costs down.

Agent: For the moment let's assume that cost isn't an issue. When it comes to the benefits that you offer, what are you trying to accomplish?

Prospect: Well, I want to offer a competitive health plan that my employees can afford to participate in.

Agent: So, can you tell me a little about current participation?

Prospect: Most of my employees are on the plan because I pay 75% of the premium but almost none of them are covering dependents and I wish they would.

Agent: So, one of your goals would be to increase dependent participation. If we could do that how would that help your company?

Conversation 2 is a rough approximation of a conversation that one of my clients had with a prospect. For this client it was a big departure from his normal conversation but it resulted in a very different series of appointments. It was important to verbally remove price from the conversation in order to get the prospect focused on more important issues. Because the focus was now on increasing dependent participation and not just premium this benefit professional was able to craft a proposal that was distinctly different from his competitors. What is important is that it is up to you to initiate a conversation that moves beyond superficial issues such as premium and network, and moves to outcomes in terms of the employer's goals. You must also recognize that very often the employer does not know what his goals are or what he wants from a broker in terms of service. A meaningful conversation begins when we know how to frame our questions not in terms of what services we offer but in terms that translate those services into what they do for the prospect.

Sales Are FAB

Asking really great questions requires the ability to convert what you do into why a prospect would care about it. Most benefit professionals are great at listing all of the services that they do but absolutely terrible at helping the prospect to understand the ways that the service is going to help him. To make the most of what of all that you can do for a client you must understand a concept known as *Features, Benefits and Advantages*.

Features

Features are simply statements of fact about your product or service. They are neither good nor bad; they are simply what they are. In the case of a major medical policy some of the features are:

- Deductibles
- Co-pays
- Co-insurance
- Lifetime maximum
- Covered expenses
- Network providers

As a prospect I may judge a $5000 deductible as a bad choice but the deductible itself is what it is. It is important to know all of the features of the plans that we sell, but not so that we can list them for the prospect. Many of the features are essentially irrelevant to the decision-making process. As an example let's consider the network on a managed care plan. It might be important to let a prospect know if one of the local hospitals is not on the plan but it is not necessary to review the entire list of providers.

Benefits

Benefits tell the prospect what a particular feature does for him. This is the reason he should care about it. The benefit of the $5000 is that the prospect can now get long-term cost control of his health plan. Most benefit professionals would have simply said that the benefit of the higher deductible is a lower cost. But while true, that answer does nothing to tell the prospect why he should care about the lower cost. The reason that brokers have had problems selling high deductible health plans is that they focus on the savings and not on how those savings can help achieve a desired outcome beyond today.

A Health Savings Account has numerous benefits such as: insuring that you will not become a burden on your children in old age, securing your retirement, and lower taxes. An idea such as "making your employees better consumers" is not a benefit. If the company is large enough to be rated on its own merits the concept of reducing the premiums may be viable but that is still not a benefit. But if reducing costs is possible then a benefit might be that the employer can improve employee morale because dependent coverage will be affordable.

A common misconception has to do with services that you may provide such as COBRA administration or the hidden paycheck. These are not benefits! Most agents believe that when they tell an employer that they will provide COBRA administration at no charge they are conveying a benefit. Unfortunately, the employer does not stop and think: "Oh Boy! That means that I no longer have to worry about the legal liability." The same thing applies to employee benefit communications. I have heard a broker tell a client that he will sit down and review all of the benefits that are currently provided as well as their value. But that statement is simply a list of features, not benefits. As a benefit professional you must convert that statement into the reasons that the employer will care about. Communicating the value of the benefits will reduce pressure for a wage increase. Now that is a benefit that an employer can identify with! Making sure that employees understand their benefits will improve morale and decrease turnover. Now it is time for you to do some work. Complete the worksheet on page 27 for as many of your products and services as possible.

Advantages

Knowing the benefits is not enough to develop an objection-free presentation because you still do not know if any of them are important to your prospect. Understanding the benefits may reduce employee turnover but if turnover isn't a concern of the employer the benefit is irrelevant. We use the benefits to craft really good questions the answers of which will provide a roadmap to the objection-free presentation. This is a critical point to understand. It is one thing to ask an employer: "Would you be interested in COBRA administration at no cost?" Only an idiot would say no to a free service but that does not mean that he cares about it. I get calls on a regular basis from brokers that have purchased one of the online agency management systems such as MyBasic Guru or ZyWave and are finding that their clients are not utilizing the tools available. More importantly, these services are not impacting either their prospect-to-client conversion ratios or their retention rate. This is because they never asked the right questions to discover whether these tools would have value. As an example, rather than ask if the prospect would be interested in free COBRA administration I might ask: "Would an idea that can minimize your legal liability be of interest to you?" If the prospect replies affirmatively I can now position COBRA in a way that matters to the prospect. If the prospect explicitly states that this is important, I now have an advantage.

Advantage

Links a benefit to an explicitly stated goal of the prospect

Advantages are used in the presentation of your solution. You would begin by stating the feature of a product or a service that you are going to provide: "As part of my service I will provide free COBRA administration." You link this to a benefit such as: "The benefit of this is that it will reduce the workload on your human resource department." Finally, you link back to an explicitly stated goal of the prospect: "This will help you achieve your goal of not having to hire another human resource assistant." The key is that the prospect **must have** stated the goal. If the prospect did not state that avoiding having to hire another person in human resources was important then you do not have an advantage. It is the ultimate linkage to explicitly stated goals that create the objection-free presentation.

There is one more very important benefit of identifying the benefits of your products and services and that is in helping you define and identify the *High Quality Prospect*. In the next chapter we will investigate the role that benefits have in helping you identify these prospects.

Homework Lesson 1

Complete the worksheet for your core products and services

Features and Benefit Worksheet

Product of Service	Features	Benefit
		Why it matters

LESSON 2

WORKING WITH THE

HIGH QUALITY PROSPECT

Previously you were introduced to the concept that selling benefits is really about helping the prospect make a decision to implement a change. When the benefit professional focuses on what **he believes** is the needs or problems of the prospect the end result will be objections. The goal is to identify what the prospect wants to accomplish and then position our solution in terms of achieving those outcomes. Before you can focus on what someone wants you must have an appointment. In traditional sales training salespeople are taught that it is about getting as many appointments as possible. The theory is that the more appointments you have the more sales that you will make. It is hard to argue with that logic. After-all you cannot hit a home run if you never get up to bat. Following that logic the salesperson is taught that if the prospect says: "I am not interested, thank you" the correct response is to attempt to overcome the objection. The most common objection-handling technique taught is the Feel, Felt, Found formula. This where the salesperson replies with: "I understand how you feel. In fact many of my current clients felt exactly the same way at first but after giving me a chance they found that my ideas had merit and could in-fact save them money." This is what I know for sure about that technique:

1. You will get some appointments
2. Less than 10% will convert into a client
3. One-third of them will be no-shows
4. Creating proposals for these appointments is a lot of work

It just doesn't make sense in today's environment to waste time with prospects that really have no interest in what you are offering.

Change Theory and Prospecting

There are a variety of different change models available as a basis for helping people make the decision to implement change. I first came into contact with the concept of change as a sales model when I went through the Certified MasterStream Instructor program in 2002. Developed by T. Falcon Napier, MasterStream was based on the idea that there were five levels of Tension that indicated one's readiness to change. T. Falcon Napier identified these levels of Tension as: Apathy, Power-Apathy, Power, Power-Stress and Stress. The concept of the sales process being about implementing change just intuitively seemed to be the missing piece in managing the sales process. For the purpose of identifying high quality prospects and recognizing whether a prospect was ready to close, the concept of change management just made sense. From that introduction I began to research change management in earnest. The first and the most widely used Change Model is The Transtheoretical Change Model developed by James O. Prochaska, PH.D., John C. Norcross, PH.D., Carlo C. DiClemente, PH.D. et al, and was developed in the 1970s and first used to deal with smoking cessation. Over time the model has been applied to a variety of addiction such as alcohol abuse, drug addiction and even eating disorders. It has even been adopted by the Centers for Medicaid and Medicare to develop tailored interventions to increase participation in informed health plan choice among Medicare beneficiaries. The Transtheoretical Change Model (TTM) identified six stages of change labeled as: pre-contemplation, contemplation, preparation, action, maintenance and termination. For more information I suggest reading Changing For Good, or using Google and reading the many resources available on the internet. After reading the Transtheoretical Change Model I immediately saw many similarities to the MasterStream stages of tension. Another model that intrigued me was by Richard Beckhard and Rueben T. Harris that dealt with overcoming resistance to change. They stipulated that there were three steps to overcoming resistance to change and they were: Dissatisfaction with the present, vision of what is possible in the future and achievable first steps towards reaching this vision. One other model worth noting is Jeffrey Hiatt's ADKAR model of change. In the ADKAR model you have the following:

Awareness of the need to change
Desire to support and participate in change
Knowledge of how to change
Ability to implement the desired skills and behaviors
Reinforcement to sustain the change

While on the surface there may appear to be differences, they are all pretty similar. The importance of understanding change theory is that if we can identify where an individual is as it applies to readiness to change, we can tailor our approach to help move the process forward.

As I studied Change Theory I recognized that from a sales perspective a prospect can be identified as being in one of five stages of readiness to implement a change.

Sales Stage #1

In Stage 1 the prospect has absolutely no interest in making a change. In fact this prospect is completely unaware that that there are options that can help improve his situation. More importantly he is happy with the status quo and has no interest in wasting time looking at options. This is the "If it ain't broke don't fix it" mentality. A prospect may be at this level for a number of reasons. The prospect may actually be very happy with the way things are and sees risk in implementing any change and is not willing to accept that risk. This is the prospect that would decline an offer to exchange a $5 bill for a $10 bill because he is sure there is something wrong with the offer. This prospect may have been working with the same broker for 20 years and trusts that is there was anything of value in the benefits market this broker would bring it to him.

The important thing to know about the Sales Stage 1 prospect is that the likelihood of making a sale is very, very small. This is not to say that once in a while you will not make a sale, but in the overall scheme of things the amount of work involved in quoting this prospect does not justify the time spent on low likelihood prospects. Recently, after a half-day program one of the benefit professionals in the room approached me to share the following story. He had met the president of a large company at a networking event and was able to secure permission to call him about a group term life and disability income program that was specifically designed for his industry. During the follow-up telephone call the president referred him to the CFO as the person to talk with about this idea. After several attempts the broker finally got through to the CFO and was told that he had no interest in working with any other brokers. Like the good salesperson that he is Steve used every objection-handling technique in his portfolio to obtain an appointment. As it turns out one of the objections was that this CFO had worked with the same agent for over twenty years and had no interest in working with anyone else. Finally, the CFO agreed to send Steve a census and other necessary information with the understanding that Steve would have a complete proposal for their meeting, which Steve agreed to. The day of the appointment Steve and his partner excitedly appeared at the scheduled appointment sure that once this CFO saw how much work they put into this proposal and the value of this idea the sale would be consummated. Well, the CFO agreed that this was actually a very good idea and was worth looking into further. Unfortunately for Steve the next sentence sealed his personal fate when the CFO told him that his agent of twenty years said that he could get appointed with this carrier and implement the program for him. Steve made the sale but lost the case! This prospect was obviously at Stage 1 and not worthy of an appointment. I know that every benefit professional reading this has had a similar case where the prospect took your ideas to his current broker.

Sales Stage #2

The prospect in Stage 2 really does not want to schedule an appointment but will be happy to receive something in the mail or via email. Like the prospect in

Stage 1 the likelihood of converting to a client by getting an appointment is very low. In many cases the prospect that requests information be mailed is using the request as a smoke screen to get rid of you without being rude. None-the-less sending information by either email or regular mail is not a bad idea. Email is preferable since there is no cost involved but either way you must secure permission to follow-up. The benefit of sending information is that you may spark real interest and move the prospect to Sales Stage 3 where there is at least a chance of making a sale.

Sometimes there is a legitimate request for information by a prospect who wasn't really considering any change but likes the idea that you presented. To verify the veracity of the request you can ask for permission to get some information. If the prospect is simply using the request to have information sent to him as a smoke screen there will be resistance to giving you any information beyond address and telephone number. On the other hand, if there is real interest the prospect will share the number of employees and some basic benefit information. In the event that the prospect refuses your request to ask a few questions you should ask if the prospect is simply trying to be nice rather than telling you to take a hike. This breaks the ice, gets an honest answer and may leave the door open for future contact.

With prospects in both Stage 1 and Stage 2 there is an alternative option which will help develop your brand over time. Ask every one of these prospects if you can add them to your monthly email newsletter. In the section on marketing I will address how to develop a valuable email newsletter but for now suffice it to say that you want to add every prospect to your newsletter distribution.

Sales Stage #3

The prospect in Sales Stage 3 will respond to your attempts to secure an appointment by saying: "That sounds interesting. Sure I would love to meet with you about that." This prospect is open to making to a change and believes that your idea has enough merit to justify scheduling time in his calendar for you. There is no guarantee that you will make a sale but the door is open enough that you know there is a relatively high probability that this prospect will implement change sometime in the near future. If you are one of those brokers that secure renewal dates and call for an opportunity to quote, this is the prospect that opens the books for multiple brokers. Being allowed to quote does not imply that the prospect is going to change but that he is open to the idea that the incumbent may not be providing the best options.

Sales Stage #4

The prospect is Sales Stage 4 is ready to implement a change. He as actually made the decision to implement change and simply needs a strategy. This prospect responds to your approach by saying: "I need to do something and soon, so let's get together." This is often seen by the benefit professional as the prospect that has gotten numerous proposals but says: "If you can get something together by next week I will be happy to give you a shot but I have to make a decision by then." It is apparent that a decision is imminent and that change is going to occur. Contrast that response with another regularly heard from a prospect in a similar situation: "Look, I have already gotten a number of proposals and I am pretty sure that I going to stay with my current broker. What can you show me that the other brokers could not?" This response is a clear Sales Stage 2. Unless there is something that you can offer that is dramatically different than your competitors, scheduling an appointment would be a waste of time.

Sales Stage #5

Sales Stage 5 is actually a full circle moment because it is identical to Sales Stage 1. In Stage 5 the prospect has already implemented a change and now wants to review the change and learn whether it was a good choice. This prospect will respond to your inquiry with: "We just changed health plans (or we went with a new broker) and are happy with our decision." Since it requires a lot of energy on the part of this prospect to change it is highly unlikely that you can convince this prospect to make a move. For practical purposes this prospect is hoping to maintain the status quo for a little while. The change required a new enrollment, new deductions, new forms and perhaps getting to know the processes of the new broker. As in Stages 1 and 2 the best approach to this prospect is to obtain permission to add him to your newsletter.

This chart outlines the different stages of change in each of the various change models.

Description	Transtheoretical Change	Beckhard & Harris	Masterstream	ADKAR	Mel's Stage Theory
I am happy with things as they are	Precontemplation	N/A	Apathy	N/A	1
I might be open to reading about this	Contemplation	Dissatisfaction	Power Apathy	Awareness	2
I need to do something so let's gather data and make a plan	Contemplation & Action	Vision of the possibilities	Power	Desire to support change and Knowledge to implement	3
I need to do something and I am going to take action	Action	Achievable first steps	Power - Stress	Ability to implement	4
I need to take of this right now – help!	N/A	N/A	Stress	N/A	N/A
Let's see how this works out	Maintenance	N/A	Apathy	Reinforcement to sustain change	5

If you could fill your calendar with prospects in any of these stages there is no doubt that you would want them all to be stage 3 or 4. In fact, you can fill your calendar with high quality prospects.

The High Quality Prospect

As you can see from the previous section it is very easy to spend a lot of time with prospects who are highly unlikely to become your client. Your goal should be to fill your calendar with appointments that have a high probability of converting to a client. The first step of course is to identify the qualities of the high quality prospect because until you know what one looks like it will be particularly difficult to fill your calendar with them.

The High Quality Prospect has four qualities:

The prospect knows the exact idea that you are coming to talk about:

This is a critical component to the high quality prospect. Too often brokers secure appointments by asking for an appointment to stop by and "introduce our services" to the prospect. This is not an idea and while you may get the appointment you will not make a sale. Permission to quote is not an idea and neither is "saving money" on your health plan. An idea is a statement about a concept that can help the prospect achieve some goal. If I call an employer and state that I have an idea that has helped many of my clients minimize or eliminate next year's rate increase, and he schedules time in his calendar for me, there is a specific idea for the meeting.

Ideas are derived from your list of features and benefits. Generally your benefits are the basis of your ideas. If I provide COBRA administration and assume regulatory liability I can call a prospect and say: "I have an idea that can minimize your regulatory liability as it pertains to employee benefits." Again, if the prospect likes the idea we have a basis for a high quality appointment.

The prospect has an interest in that idea:

The important thing here is that you did not have to overcome an objection to get the appointment. If the prospect readily gave you the appointment it is probably that your prospect is in Sales Stage 3 or 4. If you had to overcome an objection it is likely that:

- The prospect will not buy
- The prospect will be a no-show
- You will be relegated to a non-decision-maker or a non-influencer

The prospect that has no interest in your idea is fine so long as you get permission to add him to your newsletter and follow-up periodically.

The prospect is open to make a change:

Think back to the story about Steve in the last section. The prospect told him that he had been with the same agent for 20 years and had no interest in working with anyone else. Even though Steve obtained the appointment the prospect had told him that he was not going to change. The prospect must agree that he is open to implementing a change. This does not mean that you are getting a promise of business. A prospect may say: "I will be happy to meet with you about this idea. I cannot promise that I will do anything but I will certainly hear you out." This prospect is telling you that you have a shot at the business if you can convince him that you can do what you say you can do. This prospect is a clear Sales Stage 3 and is definitely worth the time and energy necessary.

The prospect is in a position to make a decision to change:

While not an absolute requirement it is important to try to get your appointments with the people that can make a decision to change. Too often benefit professionals ask for the person who handles the insurance. Most of the time this is not only **not** the decision-maker, but it is not even the person that can recommend a change. At the very least the appointment must be with a person high enough on the food chain to influence change. The easiest way to insure that you are always dealing with people at this level is to ask for the owner or president of a company. If this person refers you down to someone else, it is likely a person with influence. In larger companies you may want to begin by asking for the V.P of Human Resources or the CFO. An appointment with any person at a lower level will result in your proposal being viewed as a commodity rather than an idea that has merit and can help the company.

Understanding the different stages of change will make a huge difference in how you prospect and set appointments. In my opinion the sole objective of a great marketing program is to identify those prospects that are open to and ready for change and obtain appointments with them. It is critical that you understand that great selling skill is not about making somebody buy a product that they have no interest in. Great selling is about finding people who can see that there is a benefit in talking with you.

Homework for Lesson 2

1: Make some prospecting calls and see if you can identify what sales stage the prospect is in.

2: If you have a scheduled first appointment with a new prospect try to identify what sales stage he is in. Immediately after the call write down what the prospect said that supports the sales stage.

LESSON 3

THE INITIAL CONTACT

The employee benefit sale like most sales must go through a series of different stages. As I see it the benefit professional begins with the initial contact, moves to information gathering, presentation and finally scheduling the enrollment. It is possible to have an initial contact that automatically transitions directly into information gathering although I think that this is not only unlikely but counter-productive for all but the smallest of groups. The presentation should under all conditions be a scheduled next step. Each stage of the process has a set of goals. Achievement of the goals for each stage of the process sets up a successful transition to the next stage and ultimately to the objection-free close.

The Initial Contact

An Initial contact is as the name implies the first contact that you have with a new prospect. The contact may occur as a result of a door-to-door cold call, a telemarketing call, a direct mail response, or any other source including a referral. Prior to your call this person may not have a clue that change is in the future. The employer, who is a referral and knows you are going to call, is still relatively sure that change is not going to occur. At this point in time there is little sense of urgency and the prospect sees little value in changing (see figure 5-1).

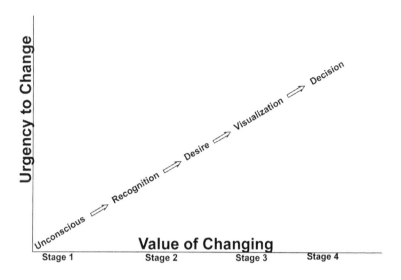

Figure 3-1

If your approach included an idea that grabbed the prospect's attention he may move from complete unconsciousness to a modicum of recognition that there is some reason to invest time in meeting with you. As you enter the initial contact you have four goals.

Ignite Interest

Your first goal is to ignite interest. To do this you use an idea from your list of benefits as a conversation opener. As a benefit professional you should have at a minimum ten great ideas that you can share with a prospect. You might have started the conversation with: "I have an idea that can help you reduce employee pressure for increased wages" or "Would you be interested in an idea that can help you get control of benefit costs?" You want the prospect to acknowledge the value of your proposition and allow you to ask questions that will fan the flames of his desire to move forward.

Focusing on saving money may get you an appointment but it does little to ignite interest. I am frequently asked about this since it appears that the high cost of health insurance is a major issue – and it is a major issue. But as a starting point for a conversation it has little value because every other agent in your community claims that they can save the prospect money. Unfortunately, saving money is not possible without tweaking the plan design. If you are creative enough to tweak the plan design without sacrificing the benefits that the employees perceive, you are not saving the employer money but doing something entirely different. Rather than saving the employer money you're helping reallocate resources to get more value out the current dollars. Read both statements together and choose the one that sounds more interesting:

- ✓ I have a couple of ideas that can save you money
- ✓ I have a couple of ideas that help my client reallocate current resources so that they get more value for their dollars.

Both statements describe what you do, but the second differentiates you from your competition. More importantly, where both questions may get the employer to ask how you are going to do what you do, only the second opens the door to a discussion of the employer's objectives in offering benefits.

Qualify the Prospect

Previously, you were introduced to the concept of the High Quality Prospect. Before you schedule a next step you absolutely must identify if you are talking to someone who meets the criteria. Assuming that you have ignited interest it is imperative that you secure permission to ask a few questions. Your first question should be: "If we move forward with discussing your benefits, who else besides you needs to be involved in any decision to implement a new program?" If the person that you are speaking with claims to be the decision-maker but is not the owner or president of the company, you should ask for clarification. You clarify by asking the following question: "So, if at our next appointment you like what I present you could, if you chose, sign any contracts to move forward, correct?" While this seems harsh it is imperative that you identify the various decision-makers so that you can attempt to involve them in at least one of the follow-up appointments.

Assuming that you are focused on an idea rather than a generic "Let me introduce myself," you already have a common understanding of the reason for the visit so you must next clarify whether the prospect is open to making a change. Change may be something as simple as the prospect being open to allowing you to offer voluntary benefits or it may mean that the prospect is open to changing brokers. Many brokers go for the appointment and mistakenly believe that that serves as confirmation that the prospect is open to change. The sad truth is that many mid-level management types will sometimes schedule appointments when there is little intent on changing simply because it fills the calendar and gives the appearance of work. It is always in your best interest to ask the question: "If it looks like this idea can help you and your company, are you open to moving forward with it?" Last year I had an appointment with the Human Resource Director of a physician's office in Asheboro, North Carolina.

We had a great first meeting and scheduled a next step. Before I left I realized that I had forgotten to ask about change readiness so I stopped before leaving and asked about her openness to changing brokers. Her response was that it was highly unlikely that she would change brokers unless I could provide something that her current broker could not. After a couple of other questions I discovered that she routinely meets with brokers and if she finds an idea that is new she takes it to the incumbent because she really likes this broker. Needless to say, I cancelled the next step and added her to my newsletter.

Establish Rapport

There is an old saying that goes: "All things being equal people like to do business with people that they like. Even when things are unequal they still prefer to do business with people that they like." Before proceeding it is necessary that the prospect not only believes that you are a professional but that you are someone that he likes. Over the years I have seen an inordinate number of salespeople who were less knowledgeable than many others but were significantly more successful than their counterparts. This occurred because they were very good at creating rapport with their prospects. Some people are naturally adept at rapport building while others have to work at it. But the time spent learning the skills necessary will pay dividends for a long time to come.

Schedule an Information Gathering Appointment

Assuming that you have a High Quality Prospect that is open to implementing change you must now schedule your next appointment. You will want to avoid using any of the typically manipulative techniques that are taught such as the alternative of choice close. This is where you ask the prospect if next Tuesday at 10AM works or would Wednesday at 3PM be better? To avoid the appearance of sales manipulation simply ask the prospect to take out his appointment calendar so that you can schedule the next appointment. As a general rule the prospect that is interested will gladly oblige. Then simply ask what works for him next week. If you have times that are already booked you could simply say: "What is your availability next week? I am free any day except Tuesday or Wednesday morning." Letting the prospect choose a day accomplishes two very important tasks. First, if the prospect chooses a date from his calendar the likelihood of a no-show is minimized since you left the door open for the prospect to refuse an appointment. Second, the readiness with which the prospect responds is a great measure of the interest aroused in your ideas. With the next appointment scheduled the final steps are to send a thank you note for the time that you were given and an email confirming the scheduled appointment.

Marketing

Of course before you have to worry about the goals of the initial contact you must have a system in place that actually makes contact with prospects. This system of making contact with prospects is generically referred to as marketing.

For most Employee Benefit professionals marketing consists of either collecting renewal dates or waiting for a prospect to call because they just received a rate increase and asked a colleague who they use and like. As a side note this is not to be confused with obtaining a referral which is a completely different animal. Neither of these approaches to lead generation constitutes marketing. Renewal dates will ultimately result in appointments but they will be based on saving money which is very transactional. More importantly, an appointment based on renewal dates fails to meet the criteria of the "High Quality Prospect. As you may remember a High Quality Prospect has the following criteria:

1. The prospect knows the exact idea that you are coming to talk about. Saving money on a health plan or shopping the market are not ideas. An idea might be a strategy that will help you get control of your costs and possibly eliminate next year's rate increase.
2. The prospect has an interest in your idea. Since price is not an idea there is nothing to have interest in. It is also worth remembering that if you had to overcome an objection to secure the appointment, there is not real interest.
3. The prospect must be open to making a change. Obviously, if it is really about price (though it generally is not) the prospect is open to making a change for a lower price.
4. The prospect must be in a position to make the decision to change. If you are not meeting with a decision-maker or at the very least a strong recommender this requirement cannot be met.

In a nutshell, marketing is about creating a multi-pronged plan to attract High Quality Prospects and securing appointments with them. A multi-pronged plan will include three or more marketing tools aimed at two or more target markets. It is not enough to simply sit on the telephone collecting renewals dates and then securing opportunities to quote on their health plans. First, quoting is extremely time intensive. Even if you have a staff person who takes the data that you collected and sends out the request for proposals to every carrier in your market, it still occupies too much of your time. You must first meet with each prospect that you will be quoting. If you are not meeting with each prospect but simply requesting that the prospect email or fax the data to you, you are not an employee benefit professional. In fact, you are less efficient from the prospect's point of view than simply using the internet. After the appointment you must ensure that you have received complete information and then after reviewing all of the quotes, you must choose the appropriate one for your prospect. Finally you must meet with your prospect to review the proposal. All of this takes an enormous amount of your time and energy.

> **In a nutshell, marketing is about creating a multi-pronged plan to attract High Quality Prospects and securing appointments with them.**

The Marketing Tools

Marketing is about actively using different tools to attract enough High Quality Prospects to keep your calendar filled. Over the course of the next several pages we will take an in-depth look at thirteen different marketing tools that you can employ to fill your calendar to overflowing. Take a few minutes and review my list of marketing tools and identify those that you have used in the past.

1) Direct mail
    a) Drip mail
    b) Form Letters
    c) Flyers
    d) Direct Mail House
2) Telemarketing
    a) Outsourcing
    b) Script development
3) Speaking
    a) Client Seminars and Workshops
    b) Invitation
    c) Civic Clubs
    d) Trade Associations / Chambers
4) Trade Show
    a) Exhibiting
    b) Attending
5) E-Marketing
    a) Newsletters
    b) Website
    c) SEM
    d) E-Mail
6) Advertising
    a) Print
    b) Radio
7) Business Cards / Multi-Media
8) Networking
    a) Paid Networking (BNI)

    b) Chamber
    c) Other Gatherings
  9) Referrals
10) Client Appreciation Event
11) Writing
12) Public Relations / Media
13) Cold Calling

For the great majority of readers the list of marketing tools that they have used will consist of cold calls, telemarketing and direct mail; of these three, telemarketing for renewal dates will be the most widely used. A fairly large number of you believe that you also make great use of referrals but as you will learn in the section on referral gathering, what you generally call a referral is nothing more than the equivalent of a Yellow Pages inquiry. A great marketing program consists of implementing at least three if not more of these tools.

Your choice of marketing tools should rely heavily on identifying those techniques that resonate with your personality. In my case I really dislike cold calls so I would not put it high on my list of preferred marketing tools. On the other hand I find it easy to make a cold call if I am already out on an appointment so I build that into my overall marketing strategy. In building my coaching business I have relied on the following marketing tools: speaking, writing, direct mail, e-marketing and advertising. When I was focused on building my payroll deduction business (worksite marketing) I incorporated a large amount of telemarketing, direct mail, limited cold calling, speaking and networking to fill my calendar. To minimize the cold call nature of my telemarketing I often combined direct mail with it. At one time I also hired a full time staff person whose primary responsibility was telemarketing for me.

In creating your marketing program begin by asking yourself which of these you actually like doing. With your list in hand the next step is to prioritize the various tools in terms of which are the most enjoyable. Your next step is to identify the markets that you are interested in working with. As an Employee Benefit Professional you may choose to identify your target markets by number of employees, by industry or by geographic area. You will want to identify more than one target market. For example, you may identify both the Home Health Care business and the Automobile Dealers as target markets. In addition, you may choose to focus on those industries on a statewide basis while simultaneously building a marketing program focused on companies of 20 employees to 199 employees in the county in which you reside.

At this point I know the marketing tools that I like as well as the industries that I intend to focus my efforts on. The next step is to look at each tool and identify how to use it to reach each target market. I may decide that I will seek speaking opportunities at the annual statewide meeting of the professional associations for each identified industry. I may also use a combination of direct mail and telemarketing to go to these industries. For local businesses, I will focus exclusively on direct mail, cold calls and networking to fill my calendar. It is extremely important to know what you want each marketing tool to accomplish. Even though you may ultimately want to secure an appointment that may not be the initial objective of your marketing program. A wellness program that I worked with utilized both direct mail and telemarketing in a call – mail – call program. The principle of the company would contact the vice president of Human Resources and simply ask for permission to send some information about his wellness program. With permission granted he would send out the informational piece as well as an email immediately after the call reminding the prospect to be on the lookout for the information packet. Three days later he would follow-up with a telephone call to ask if the material was received. As you can see, the goals for the first and third calls were completely different. Even the goal for the direct mail piece was not to obtain an appointment but to ignite enough interest to motivate the prospect to want to speak to him further about employee wellness.

Before we move on to the individual marketing tools there is one other aspect of your plan that needs attention and that is the amount of time and money that you want to commit to each marketing tool. In the above scenario this is a very important question. From a financial perspective we know that the printing of brochures as well as the postage for mailing will take money. If postage on 100 pieces of mail costs $44.00 and the brochures cost approximately $1.00 each in lots of 1000 brochures, knowing my budget beforehand is critical. A total budget of $2500 for this campaign will dictate that if I send out 100 pieces per week I will be limited to a 17 week program. But time is also an issue that must be thought about. How many hours per day will I commit to telemarketing prospects seeking permission to mail this information? If I will only commit two hours per day on Monday, Tuesday and Wednesday to telemarketing that will impact my expectations of the program. If I assume that I can secure permission to send out 4 brochures per day (12 per week) then perhaps I may want to allocate some of the $2500 budget to other tools.

As you read on consider which of these marketing tools sound like those that you can and should be using to build your business. Know how many new first appointments you would like to have each week and which of these tools will resonate with your target markets. Then build your Client Creation System.

Homework for Lesson 3

1: Create a list of ideas that can be used to ignite interest

Immediately after you make an initial contact with a prospect review it in terms of the goals outlined in this section. How well did you do in meeting these objectives? Where could you have improved?

What challenges did you encounter in trying to meet the objectives?

LESSON 4

COLD CALLING

A cold call is any personal contact that you initiate with a prospect who has no prior relationship with you. Cold calling may be done in person, via the telephone or while on an airplane. Regardless of what other marketing tools you are incorporating into your overall marketing plan, cold calling should have a prominent role. For the group health agent cold calling ought to be as easy as falling off of a rock. Virtually every business that you pass is a potential prospect. If a business has health insurance it is through an agent and that agent might as well as be you. If they do not have health insurance they probably should, but they need a good agent to help them. If you are not calling on these businesses you are doing yourself and the business owners a disservice.

I am often asked two very interesting questions which must be answered if you are to understand the true value of the cold call. The first question is whether or not a veteran agent with a large client base and many referrals ought to engage in cold calling. To that I answer with an unequivocal "Absolutely!" That is not to suggest that the veteran agent should spend hours engaged in cold calling but it is to suggest that the veteran agent should incorporate some amount of cold calling into his daily or weekly activity. Cold calling accomplishes a number of very important objectives for the veteran agent.

1. It keeps the agent's selling skills fresh. The ability to engage a total stranger in a meaningful

conversation that results in new business is an incredibly valuable skill. When we rely on referrals as the sole source of our new business we risk a prolonged period of sales inactivity. Inactivity breeds complacency and that can be the agent's downfall. More importantly, most agents are not consciously asking for referrals but are relying on word of mouth to generate call-ins. As I pointed out in the section on referral gathering, there is a distinct difference between asking for referrals and hoping that clients will tell their friends about you. When you are confident in your cold calling skills you are also more likely to ask for the referral.

2. It is a new business driver. Think about the last time that you were on a sales appointment that resulted in either a sale or at the very least moved forward to a second step. Immediately after that appointment how did you feel? If you are like most salespeople you felt really good. You probably felt a surge of energy. The same feeling occurs after a successful cold call. When a cold call results in either a sale or an appointment you feel like you could conquer the world. Success breeds success and soon you have more first appointments than you have had in years.

3. It keeps the agent in control of his own destiny. As you fill your pipeline with fresh prospects you realize how much more in control you are. If you are not cold calling you are relying on outside influences to create business opportunities. If you use direct mail you are relying on a recipient to respond. The same applies to advertising. The person viewing your advertisement must take action and contact you. Even public

speaking and writing articles rely on someone else taking action. In cold calling it is the agent that takes the action. The better you are at it the more likely that a call will result in an appointment.

The second question deals with whether or not in-person cold calling is the best use of the agent's time. Agents who rely primarily on telephone prospecting often ask this question. Their concern is that when they telemarket they can cover a lot of ground quickly and if a business owner is not in, it has no real affect on their productivity. On the other hand, if they are making an in-person cold call and the business owner or other decision maker isn't in, there is a time cost for that call. The short answer is that the concern is 100% valid. The opportunity to cost for in-person cold calling is very high and for that reason I do not recommend it as a primary activity. In-person cold calling is an excellent adjunct to telemarketing cold calls and direct mail. In-person cold calling is not so much a scheduled event as it is a planned after-appointment or fill-in activity.

Successful Cold Calling

Regardless of whether we are talking about in-person or telephone cold calls, there are certain ingredients for success. Like baking a cake, if you omit any of the ingredients your cake will not turn out right. You may still end up with something that looks like a cake but it will not taste right. The same rule applies in cold calling. If you leave out any of the ingredients you may get appointments but you will definitely be working harder than the agent that includes each ingredient.

Ingredients of a Successful Cold Call

- ✓ A good prospect list – As in direct mail, a good list can make your life easier. There is no doubt that you can open up the telephone book or the Chamber of Commerce directory and begin to make calls, but you have no idea who the decision maker is or even if the company is locally owned. How much easier it is when you can ask for the owner by name.
- ✓ A strong opening statement – Yes, we are back to the strong opening statement again. As in networking and advertising, being able to translate what you do into what it means to the prospect is hugely important.
- ✓ A prepared script – The cold call is no place to try to wing it. You want to be able to provide a compelling reason for the prospect to make time to meet with you and you want to do it in as few words as possible.

Steps to a Successful Cold Call

Ask for the business owner by name: This is why a good list is so important. Consider these two openings:

"May I speak with the business owner please?"

"May I speak with Jimmy Smith please?"

In response to the first opening the gatekeeper will ask: "What is this about?" As soon as you say "group insurance," the gatekeeper will respond with, "Bill H. Remy handles that, one moment." You have now been relegated to the HR department. On the other hand in response to the second approach the gatekeeper will simply ask: "Whom may I say is calling?" and then put you through. It is critical that you ask for the business owner or president of the company. Regardless of employee size you will always want to begin at the "C" level. There are a number of reasons for this approach.

a) If you begin with human resources or the person that handles the insurance there is almost no chance of getting the decision makers involved in the discussion. Mid level managers have a vested interest in protecting their turf and are generally risk-averse. This has critical implications for your success. If the HR or insurance manager recommends that the owner or president work with you and that does not turn out well, it is the HR or insurance manager that will be held accountable. That is a big risk.

b) If the "C" level contact refers you down to a mid level manager, that manager must report back to the "C" level contact. That fact makes it easier to involve the "C" level contact in the presentation since it is now in the mid level manager's best interest to ask for their participation.

c) If your idea resonates with the "C" level contact, he is much more likely to want to participate in discussing your idea.

Start with a strong opening statement: Too many agents rely on asking for renewal dates as their cold call script. Their approach sounds like this: *"Hello, may I speak with the person that handles your group insurance please? / Hi Mr. Group Administrator, do you normally put your plan out for bid at renewal? Great! And when is that? So would it be all right to call you 90 days prior to that? Thanks so much."* The problem with that approach is that you did not offer anything other than getting a quote, which translates into a price issue. In addition, you did not offering a compelling reason to meet with you right now.

A strong opening statement is about something that you can do for your prospect right now. It is an idea which helps the prospect achieve an objective that would be of benefit to him but that he is currently missing. The strong opening statement is about changing the nature of the sales conversation from one of shopping rates to one of helping the prospect achieve his goals. Your new approach might sound like this: *"Hello, may I speak with business owner? / Ms. Owner, I work with employers in the area and help them improve their bottom line by improving employee morale and productivity. Best of all I accomplish this without any increase in cost to you. I do not know if this will work for you but I would love 10 minutes of your time to see if I can be of value."* Can you see the difference in the two approaches?

Know your script: It will be a rare event when a business owner will grant you an appointment simply because you have an idea that sounds good. The more likely response to "I have an idea about something" will be to ask for more information. In the example above, a likely response would be, "How do you accomplish that?" If you do not have a script to follow you will miss an opportunity to convert to an appointment. You might respond with: *"That is a very good question, but before I answer can I ask you a couple of quick questions?"* Since information is the currency that we deal in we must know a few things such as whether there is a health insurance plan and do his employees appreciate the value of that plan. Your response must be internalized so that you can answer the question and it sounds natural.

Your first goal is an appointment: Your prospect will try to get you to launch into a premature presentation. He will ask for specifics as to how you can accomplish your magic. Avoid at all costs a presentation during your cold call. To successfully avoid a premature presentation follow these steps:

Step #1: Respond with: "That is a very good question." This simple statement acknowledges the validity of the query. By acknowledging the query you will put the prospect at ease.

Step #2: Follow with: "In order to make my reply meaningful to you." This statement begins to give context to your next request.

Step #3: Ask for permission to ask a few questions. "May I ask you few questions?"

Step #4: Ask the questions

Step #5: Tie your response to the prospect's answers to your questions.

Let's look at a sample dialogue

Agent: Ms. Prospect, my name is Joe Agent and I have some ideas that have helped many of my clients get control of their health insurance premiums and minimize or even eliminate rate increases for up to three years. I do not know if you have an interest in getting control of your premiums but if so, may I ask you a couple of questions?
Prospect: How are you going to eliminate rate increases?

Agent: That's a very good question. In order to make my response meaningful to you may I ask you two quick questions?

Prospect: Sure

Agent: If I could help you eliminate rate increase for two to three years what would that mean to you and your company?

Prospect: Well for one thing it would help me in my annual budgeting process.

Agent: And one more question, in your opinion which is more important – the actual plan design that I present to you or your employee's perception of that plan design?

Prospect: Well I believe that how my employees perceive the plan design is the most important factor.

Agent: Well, to quickly answer your question about how I can help you minimize future increases I quite frankly create an innovative plan design that maintains current benefits for the employees and then design a strategy that manages your employees perception of the plan. Any explanation beyond that would be premature until I see if this strategy will work for you. With that in mind, do you have any time next week for brief 20 minute meeting?

As with everything in the Objection Free Selling System, everything is done in a manner that communicates that it is all about the prospect. This is a great way to begin to differentiate yourself from your competitors. You can reply to the request for information right now that you are not like every other agent that this business owner has met. You cannot tell him how you can help him improve productivity until you know a little about his company. You are only interested in sharing a solution that will be meaningful to him and his company. What worked for your last client may be meaningless to his situation. So, with that in mind, can you schedule ten minutes next Tuesday?

Never ask for more than fifteen to twenty minutes: I know that you cannot deliver a meaningful presentation in fifteen minutes. But asking for an hour may be more than a skeptical prospect wants to make available to a stranger. At the fifteen-minute mark on your first appointment you simply look at the prospect and ask how he is on time. If he is really interested in your proposition he will either continue with the conversation or be open to scheduling another appointment.

Qualify your prospect: Regardless of whether the prospect allows you two minutes or ten during the cold call, you do not want to schedule your next appointment without discovering whether or not this is high quality prospect. If nothing else you want to make sure that you are speaking with the decision maker, that there is in fact a health plan in place or if not, the prospect is willing to spend the necessary amount of money required to put a plan in place. This is a simple matter of two or three quick questions that can be asked in 45 seconds.

Scheduling Cold Call Time

If cold calling is to become second nature to you it is imperative that you allocate adequate time for it each week. It is imperative that you schedule this time into your calendar and it must be inviolate. Far too many agents think that they can get cold calling in when time permits which it inevitably never does. The group benefits business is extremely labor intensive. On any given day you have to deal with claims issues, eligibility issues, the need for duplicate ID Cards and other problems. I have heard agents tell me that they wanted to cold call but a large client called with a problem that had to be addressed. That excuse in my opinion is a cop-out. Here is the key question that you should always ask yourself: "If you had a scheduled sales appointment would you cancel it to deal with this issue?" If you would cancel a sales appointment you should not cancel your cold call time. Scheduling your cold call time and making it inviolate will result in a significant increase in your sales revenue.

Easy In-Person Cold Calls

Whenever you are out on a service or sales appointment, making an in-person cold call is an easy extension. Whenever I had a sales appointment I made it a part of my routine to always call on the two businesses on either side of my appointment and the one directly across the street.

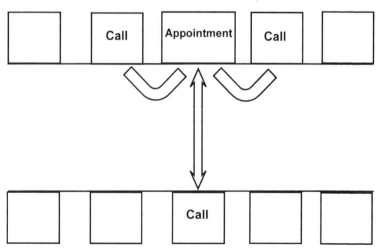

This was a relatively painless activity that resulted in numerous sales. As painless as it is, I am always amazed at how resistant group health agents are to this concept. This is a good opportunity for me to relate a true story to you. Back in 1996 I was working with Wayne, an agent from Durham, NC. Wayne had been having difficulty getting his worksite marketing business up and running and wanted to work with me for a couple of days. I subsequently dropped 500 of my dental flyers in Burlington, NC and had Wayne come to my office for a day of telemarketing. In roughly 2 hours of calling on a Tuesday I scheduled three appointments with decision-makers for that Thursday. As we finished the first call I suggested that we make three cold calls as illustrated above. On the very first call I got to meet with the president of a 50 employee printing company. I no sooner said the words voluntary dental than he wanted to schedule an appointment for later that day. At the end of the afternoon appointment I had scheduled an enrollment for both the voluntary dental and a cancer plan two weeks hence. That enrollment resulted in 40 employees enrolling in the dental plan and 25 employees enrolling in the cancer plan. The total annualized commission on the account was in excess of $5000 – all from one cold call! Unfortunately, Wayne chose to sell mobile homes rather than try to duplicate our time together.

The beauty of this strategy is that it turns every sales appointment into a minimum of one new prospect. In my experience the math works out to be one new contact with a decision maker for every appointment. For every three decision-makers I initially meet I will secure one appointment with a high quality prospect. For every 8 appointments I will convert 5 into a client. Look at all of the appointments that you had in the last 30 days and ask yourself how many new clients you would have today had you implemented this strategy.

Telemarketing Companies

There are companies out there that specialize in setting appointments for agents. Most of these companies focus on renewal dates and lowering premiums as their door opener which will certainly result in appointments. The benefit of using a telemarketing company is that it minimizes your time in the office trying to get appointments and maximizes your time doing what you do best which is selling. If you implement the above cold calling strategy you will ultimately have more business than you ever dreamed of. The drawback is that these appointments require you to be skillful at converting a discussion about price into one about the client's overall benefit objectives. This requires that you be able to **ask the right questions in the right order and at the right time**.

As you can see from this discussion, cold calling should be an integral part of your marketing program. It puts you in complete control of your destiny, because the number of appointments that you have with high quality prospects will ultimately determine how much money you make and how hard you have to work to get it.

THE CALL-EMAIL-CALL
MARKETING STRATEGY

The single biggest obstacle to a significant increase in the business of most group health producers (and for that matter most salespeople) is a lack of a new business marketing strategy. And of all the strategies available the easiest and quickest to implement is the use of "cold calling" which also happens to be the single most dreaded sales activity for most salespeople. In this article I want to share an easy to implement "Cold Call" strategy that I label: "call-email-call." I love this technique and use it in my marketing regularly. To succeed you must secure three tools: a point of sale brochure or a marketing oriented website, an email tracking tool (www.email2sell.com) and a good opening statement.

Follow these steps for amazing results.

Step 1: Identify your sales proposition
Your sales proposition is a short statement about your product or service that is designed to grab the prospect's interest. When I call prospect about my online health promotion program I open with: "I offer a revolutionary design in dental insurance that lowers premiums while increasing employee appreciation of the plan.

Step 2: Request permission to send an email
Immediately following your sales proposition you want to ask for permission to send an email. Let the prospect know that you are attaching a brochure or sending a

link to webpage where he can learn more. In my health promotion call I make the following statement: "I don't know if you have any interest but if you do may I send an email with a link to my website where you can watch a short video and learn more?" Ninety percent of these calls result in permission to send the email. Before ending the call ask for permission to send your monthly email newsletter and the month and date of the prospect's birthday. My prospect birthday list has grown like a weed since I learned this technique in January of this year.

Step 3: Send the email using a tracking service
I know that if I send this email to ten prospects only one or two will actually open the email and click on the link or open the attachment. The link tracking service notifies me as soon as the prospect opens my email and again if he opens the attachment or clicks on the embedded link. Since I hate rejection I do not have to call all ten prospects as a follow-up because I know exactly who has interest in my sales proposition

Step 4: Follow-up within sixty minutes
The beauty of tracking is that you get to follow up when interest is highest. If you wait even twenty-four hours the prospect's interest will be significantly less. It is also important not to call too soon since you do not want the prospect to feel that he is being stalked.

Most salespeople ask me about using the "Request Receipt" function in Outlook instead of the email tracking service. The problem with the "request receipt" function is that it is a request that most people ignore. More importantly, it does not tell you if the prospect actually visited your website or opened the attachment. The email tracking service on the other hand is invisible to the prospect. When I call a prospect who has clicked on the embedded link the usual response is: "Funny that you should call. I was just on your website." While every prospect may not have any further interest I still generally have a good conversation that results in a foundation for our future relationship.

Commit to getting 10 prospects per day who allow you to send them an email and I can guarantee that in 60 days you will be scheduling more sales opportunities than you ever believed possible. And since these will be very high quality appointments you will also find that you will convert a high percentage into clients.

LESSON 5

INFORMATION GATHERING

While most sales training focuses on the closing as a key skill it is my belief that sale is made or lost during the Information Gathering process. It is not your products or services that help differentiate you from the competition. Differentiation occurs in the conversation that you have with your prospect.

> *It is not your products or services that help differentiate you from the competition.*
>
> *Differentiation occurs in the conversation that you have with your prospect.*

Without a successful Information Gathering Appointment you not only will fail to get the case, you will have to deal with a lot of objections. There are seven goals for this part of the selling process.

Reestablish Rapport

Unless you and the prospect just naturally got along during the initial contact it will be important to spend some time reestablishing rapport. You should have in your notes the prospect's behavioral style so that you can review prior to the appointment. You may spend a couple of minutes in general chit-chat or you may simply remind the prospect of your last visit. Regardless of your approach to rapport building you must ensure that the prospect is comfortable with you before proceeding.

Identify and Involve Decision-Makers

If you have not already identified all of the parties to the decision-making process you will want to do this now. If possible ask for all of the parties to participate in this meeting. No doubt you have closed many, if not most of your cases by dealing with the human resource manager or a benefit clerk in the past and so may not see the need to push this issue. But if you want to be able to avoid the six dreaded words after your presentation you must include all decision-makers. There are a couple of reasons for involving all of the decision-makers here.

The Six Dreaded Words

I want to think about it

During the information gathering meeting you want to identify the prospect's goals so that you can craft a proposal that explicitly addresses them. But it is important to recognize that the goals of the president of the company are not necessarily the same goals that a human resource manager may have. The CFO will be looking at a different set of objectives than either the president of the human resources manager. If you can get them all involved in a meeting you can identify each of their goals and craft much more of an objection-free proposal.

Identify Goals and Objectives

As you may recall from Lesson 3 people are most motivated by the things that they want but do not currently have. A secondary motivator is the desire to avoid losing something that they have and value. Your goal, in fact your primary goal, is to identify the prospect's various goals so that you can present a strategy to achieve them using your products and services. Uncovering the prospect's goals is a function on how effective you are at asking the really great questions from Lesson 6.

It is critical to remember that just because a prospect may say that reducing employee turnover is important does not automatically make that a valuable goal to focus on. One of the most important aspects of identifying goals is uncovering areas of cognitive dissonance – where what the prospect says is important and what really is important are not the same thing. During the Information Gathering phase you want to go beyond the superficial and get to the heart of what really matters to the prospect.

Manage Expectations

For many of you managing expectations is going to be an alien concept. The approach that most Benefit Professionals take is to provide the prospect with a brochure or a list and review all of the services that your agency will provide. As a general rule this approach utilizes a strategy of hope rather than a thought-out consulting strategy. The list of services approach operates on the basis that one or two of your services will jump out at the prospect or that the depth of your list will somehow overwhelm the prospect and make him choose you over the competition.

The reality of how ineffective this strategy is can be seen in the number of prospects that say: "Let me review this and give me a call next week." If they were overwhelmed the prospect would not need to think about it.

Because this phase is labeled "Information Gathering" your goal is to help the prospect identify which services would be important to him. It is critical to remember what happens to your own mind when someone is talking about something that you have no interest in. Let's assume that you have no interest in the television show "Dancing with the Stars." If you and I are talking and I begin to tell you about last night's show and how Jane Seymour did, what happens to your attention to me? More than likely your mind will begin to wander. This is exactly what happens when you begin to tell your prospect about all of the wonderful services that you can provide. They stop listening not only because some of the services may not have value but because this is what every other benefit broker does. In the prospect's mind he can review these later.

Even if you can keep the prospect's attention there is one very major negative impact of this strategy. If I promise a prospect that I will visit monthly and meet with all new hires and I do exactly that, all I have succeeded in doing is meeting their expectations. But what if the prospect tells me that they want me to visit quarterly and I begin to visit every six weeks? Now I have exceeded their expectations. Which has a bigger impact in the mind of the new client? This is not "under-promise and over-deliver." In that scenario, advocated by many trainers, you manipulate the prospect. What I advocate is asking the right questions so that the prospect tells you exactly what services he wants. Once the prospect tells you exactly what he wants in the way of services you can craft a proposal that contains only that which the prospect explicitly told you was important. Your proposal will be unique because you and you alone will have a proposal focused on the prospect's goals. And once chosen as the broker you will be able to easily exceed expectations and generate an avalanche of referrals.

Raise the Prospect's Sense of Urgency

An objection-free presentation cannot be created without this step. As I said earlier the mere fact that the prospect states that a particular service has value does not automatically make it important. A prospect might actually want his employees to have a better understanding of the benefits provided but that is not the same thing as having a sense of urgency around attaining that goal. To build a sense of urgency around a particular goal we must get the prospect to elaborate on why a particular goal has value. The more that a prospect expounds on a given goal the more important that goal becomes to him. Earlier you learned about the building question and that is exactly what you use to raise the sense of urgency around any goal.

Raising the prospect's sense of urgency around a given goal is absolutely necessary before the next step can be done effectively. To understand the importance of creating urgency, think about something that you wanted, had an opportunity to purchase, but ultimately didn't. Now, think about another time when you knew that you really wanted to buy something and actually expended your energy on obtaining it. Try to identify the importance that you attached to each situation. When we really want something we will move heaven and earth to obtain it, regardless of whether we need it or not. Our actions are in direct proportion to the importance that we place on obtaining something. In the benefit selling arena we must help the prospect get in touch with the why behind every stated goal.

Eliminate the Incumbent

In my workshops I am often asked why I believe that eliminating the incumbent happens during information gathering rather than during presentation. Before answering that very important question I want to ask you one. Have you ever had following situation?

You meet with a client and discover that she is less than enthusiastic about the incumbent and uncover that the incumbent does not provide a specific service such as COBRA Administration. In addition you discover that the incumbent presents the renewal with only four weeks to go until renewal. You come back with a great proposal that saves them money and includes free COBRA administration. You also review your approach to the renewal which includes presenting the renewal numbers eight weeks prior to renewal. As you conclude your presentation you are confident that the case is yours. You ask what the prospect believes should be the next step and hear the dreaded words: "Well, let me see if my current broker can provide any of these services?"

I know that every benefit professional reading this has had that experience. It happens because you first failed to raise the prospect's sense of urgency and then did not tie the specific service to the incumbent's inability to provide this. It is absolutely critical that once a prospect tells you that something is important you ask why it is important and follow with: "So what has you current broker done to solve this issue?" If you have done a good job of raising a sense of urgency the prospect will mentally say: "That no good son of gun has never even asked me about this." It is during the information gathering phase that we help the prospect connect the dots between what they want and the incumbent's inability to address the issue.

Schedule the Next Step

Imagine that you have gotten all of the necessary information to move forward and gather proposals from the various carriers. Do you schedule the next appointment or do you leave it open and say: "As soon as I get all of the numbers in from the various carriers I will give you a call and schedule a time to get together." Ninety-nine percent of you reading this do the latter and that is too bad. When you do that some number of prospects will ask that you send it to them by mail or email. Some number will never schedule an appointment with you. Creating a proposal is a lot of work and should never be undertaken without a next step scheduled on the calendar. If the prospect refuses to schedule an appointment, that tells you volumes about the potential for getting the business. In rare instances it is possible that the prospect will have a legitimate reason for not scheduling an appointment and that is all right. But unless you ask for the appointment you do not know where you stand.

A common question that I get is about the prospect that does not have the census and other information ready. The approach that most brokers take is to have the prospect email or fax the information. Unfortunately, very often you end up calling and following up week after week in an attempt to get the data. Last year I was engaged in a sales training program with a benefit consulting firm in Raleigh, North Carolina and this issue came up. The prospect seemed very interested in having this agency work on their benefits and week after week kept promising to get the data to them and failed to follow through. I suggested that the broker responsible for this account call up the prospect and ask to schedule a brief ten minute appointment to pick up the data, which was granted. Needless to say, when the broker arrived, the data was ready.

Whether it is to pick up data or return for the presentation a scheduled appointment is a very positive indicator. It does not insure that you will get the business but it does mean that you are in a lot better shape than the brokers that did not request the appointment. And one final point about the next step. Remember earlier when I said that you can only differentiate yourself by the conversation that you have with a prospect? When you are the only benefit professional that schedules the next step you are communicating that you are not only different but also more effective than your competitors.

Managing Information Gathering

As I indicated earlier the Information Gathering phase may be a separate appointment or it may be a transition from the initial contact. In either case your first step is making the transition from rapport building to asking questions that create your roadmap for the sale. Hopefully you have identified the behavioral style of your prospect so that you can transition in terms of that. If you are working with a Type A personality (the typical business owner) you can transition by saying: "I know that you are extremely busy so if you don't mind I would like to get down to business. May I begin by asking some questions?" From the perspective of the owner or president this transition lets him know that you understand that he is incredibly busy and important and that you respect his time. If the prospect is a Human Resource Professional this reasoning holds true as well but from an entirely different perspective. Unlike the business owner or CEO the HR professional does not really care about the prestige aspect of position but does like to be recognized as having a lot of work to do. In the event that you are talking a CFO you want to acknowledge his need to gather all of the facts before making a decision.

Gather Details

There are many matters of fact that you must learn about in order to do a good job for the prospect. You must know if there is a health plan in place, if so, with what carrier and what is the plan design. You will need to know how much of the employee premium the employer pays as well as how much, if any, of the dependent premium is employer paid. Employee participation will have to be ascertained as well as the number of dependents. If there are any other employer paid benefits you will want to talk about them as well as any voluntary benefits.

Early in the sales process you will want to go through as much of the fact-finding as possible and get it out of the way. The reason that you want to get this out of the way early is simply because this part of the process has very little emotional impact. As you move into your Objective oriented questions you will begin to ignite emotion and once you do it is imperative that you do nothing that mitigates that sense of urgency. I suggest that you create a fact-finder that you can pull out that covers every aspect of employee benefits that you can think of. Ask about everything related to the benefit process regardless of whether you sell that product or not. Your goal is two-fold. First, you want to identify all areas of current opportunity that can be capitalized on during the presentation. Your second goal is to identify areas for future exploration with a strategic alliance partner.

Details

Product	Employer-paid	Employee-Paid	Interest in Offering	Not Applicable
Group Health				
Dependent Health				
Group Term Life				
Short-term DI				
Long-term DI				
Dental				
Long Term Care				
Wellness Program				
401K				
Other Retirement				
Executive Carve out DI				
SERP				
Cancer Insurance				
Accident Insurance				
Critical Illness				
Permanent Life				
Mini – Med				

Figure 6-1

You should also develop a separate fact-finder for the services that you can offer. You will want to know if the employer currently has a system in place to effectively communicate benefits or to handle COBRA or to comply with HIPAA. And while these service-related questions are detail in nature you will want to hold off asking about these until you get to the goal- oriented questions in the next section.

Building Urgency

With the details out of the way it is time to begin to identify what it is that the prospect wants to accomplish. As you identify a goal you will always follow-up with a Building Question to build a sense of urgency around that particular goal as well as to give you an idea of its importance. As you can see from Figure 6-2 the Objective Oriented Question builds desire and heightens the sense of urgency.

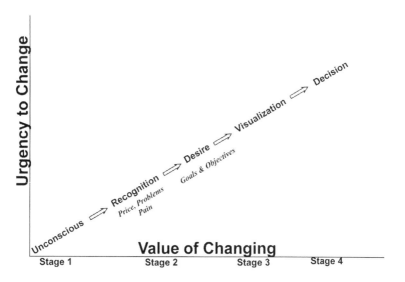

Figure 6-2

Before you begin to ask any questions about services that the prospect may want and that you can deliver you will want to revisit your list of products. If there are any products that the prospect does not currently have but has indicated an interest in looking at, you will want to ask for some clarification. If, for example, the employer did not have a dental plan in place but seemed open to discussing it, you will want to know a little more about its importance. You might have the following discussion:

You: "Mr. Employer, you indicated that you would be open to looking at adding a dental plan. Do I have that right?"

Employer: "That is correct, however I am not promising that I can pay for one."

You: "I understand that but can I ask why you have any interest in a dental plan at all?"

Employer: "Well, I know that my employees have been asking for one for quite some time now."

You: "What impact do you think a dental plan would have?"

Employer: "I think that it would make my employees happier if they had one."

As with any objective you always immediately follow with at least one building question. The question about the perceived impact of offering a dental plan is a prime example of a building question. By asking the prospect to verbalize why something is important you help him connect the dots between a goal and why that goal is important. Failure to ask the follow-up question will result in objections at the time of your presentation. You cannot assume that a positive response has any emotional value and in fact often does not. Figure 6-3 illustrates what happens as you ask these building questions.

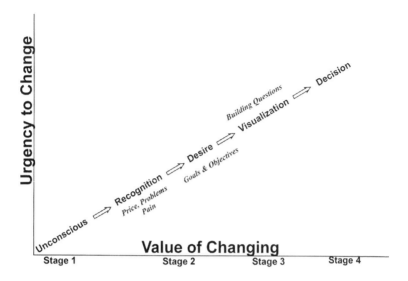

Figure 6-3

The building question creates a visualization of the rewards of achieving a particular goal, in this case adding a dental plan. What is particularly important is that it is the prospect and not the broker that states the importance of adding the benefit. Previously it was noted that – "If you say it as the salesperson, it is automatically suspect, even if true. If the prospect says it, it is automatically true, even if false." Whenever possible you want the prospect to make all connections.

One of your key goals during the information gathering phase is to eliminate the incumbent and this is the time to do that. Once you have identified a goal and successfully gotten the prospect to elaborate on its importance, you ask the Obstacle Question. Let's continue with the dialogue about dental. The employer has told us that a dental plan would make his employees happy and a good follow-up would be:

You: "Mr. Employer, how would happy employees benefit you?"

Employer: "Obviously if they are happy they will work harder."

You: "So what has kept you from implementing one?"

Employer: "Well, as I said, I cannot pay for one at this time?"

You: "Would you be open to a voluntary plan that does not require you to pay the premium?"

Employer: "Sure, but I didn't know that you could do that."

You: "Do you think that would accomplish the goal of happier employees?"

Employer: "Absolutely"

You: "So, has your current broker ever suggested a voluntary plan?"

Employer: "As a matter of fact he has never brought that up."

In this exchange you see the Obstacle Questions asked twice. The first time is when the broker asks about the reason for not pursuing a dental plan in the past. Once the broker learns that it was pursued but the employer did not want to pay the premium there is a change of direction and a voluntary plan is pursued. You see both the Objective Oriented Question followed by the building question. With agreement that a voluntary plan would work, the broker asks the obstacle question that is tied to the incumbent. Failure to ask the Obstacle Question will result in these dreaded words at point of presentation: "Well, let me ask my current broker if he can provide a voluntary dental plan." The Obstacle Question creates dissatisfaction with the status quo. Here is another example around employee benefit communications:

Broker: "Do you think that it would be of value to you if your employees had a better understanding of the benefits that you provide and their value?" (Objective Oriented Question)

Employer: "I suppose that would be beneficial."

Broker: "If your employees had a better understanding of the value of the benefits that you provide how would that benefit your company?" (Building Question)

Employer: "Well, right now they have no idea of the cost of their health insurance. I would hope that if they actually knew how much I was spending they might stop complaining about not getting a raise."

Broker: "By that you mean that it might improve morale?" (Building Question)

Employer: "That's exactly what I mean!"

Broker: "So what impact do you see improved morale having?" (Building Question)

Employer: "I would think that I would have less turn-over."

Broker: "And what has your current broker suggested as a strategy to deal with?" (Obstacle Question)

By asking a series of building questions the broker succeeds in raising the employer's sense of urgency to take some action to deal with this issue. And by asking the final Obstacle Question the broker forces the employer to acknowledge that the incumbent hasn't even asked about this issue. Figure 6-4 illustrates the effect of this line of questioning.

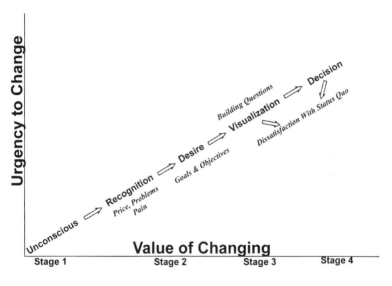

Figure 6-4

It is important to not ask the obstacle question on every single goal that you uncover. Even more importantly, do not try to tie the incumbent to every goal. You want to judiciously apply the pressure and focus on goals that seem particularly important to the prospect. The more important the goal, the more value the Obstacle Question will have.

The basic formula for Information Gathering is:

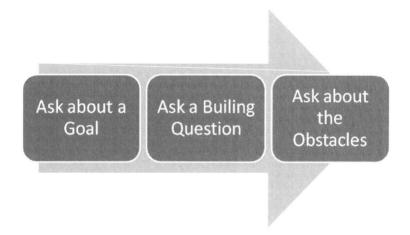

Follow this formula for each individual goal. Complete one goal before moving on to another. By focusing on one goal at a time you can easily identify which goals are very important and need to be addressed in your presentation and which carry little emotional power.

The final step of this section is to do a brief review before scheduling the next step. You simply review each goal and the reasons why they were important and ask: "Have I missed anything?" This gives the prospect a chance to correct any misunderstanding and to add to your list. In many cases there may be other issues that weren't covered and the prospect should be relatively comfortable with your effectiveness and will be extremely open with you.

Schedule the Next Step

There is nothing more important than scheduling the next step before leaving the appointment. Asking the prospect to take out his calendar and schedule the next appointment provides a key indicator of success potential. Any resistance, other than a legitimate reason such as "I would really like the President in on the next meeting and I do not have her calendar" is a strong indicator of a lost sale. If the prospect should use a common refusal to schedule a next step such as: "Well, why don't you give me a call as soon as you are ready with your proposal" you should follow-up with: "Let me ask you a quick question. I do not want to waste any of your time and I certainly do not want to waste my time doing all of the work necessary in creating a proposal, so is there a reason that you are reluctant to schedule an appointment to meet to review my recommendations?" This follow-up will uncover the level of real interest in working with you. The response might be that she wants to include her boss but it might be that she just does not want to schedule an appointment. You might even be told that this person never, ever schedules the presentation appointment until notified that the proposal is complete. If it were me I would state unequivocally: "Well, in that case I wish you the best of luck. I do not operate that way. It really does require a lot of work to get everything together and this is obviously not that important to you, but thanks for your time today." This is just a guess but I am sure that no one reading this needs any practice in shopping benefits and creating proposals.

So schedule the next step and return with an objection-free presentation.

Homework Lesson 6

Analyze you appointments in terms of how much of the time is spent with you talking versus asking questions and letting the prospect talk.

Did you obtain the necessary information so that you can craft a proposal that matches the prospect's explicitly stated goals?

LESSON 6

REALLY GREAT QUESTIONS

The key to the objection-free sale is the ability to ask really great questions. The ability to ask great questions is actually more important to your business success than knowledge of benefits. Since most benefit professionals believe just the opposite, that knowledge is what matters most, I ask you to bear with me. You see, if you ask the prospect the right questions they will tell you exactly what they want and exactly what you have to do to get their business. Give me a salesperson that can ask great questions and knows where to go to get help in creating a proposal and I will show you a salesperson that will win 90% of the time. Before we get to how to craft a really great question, let's take a look at a couple of important definitions.

Closed-Ended Questions: These are questions that can be answered without any elaboration. Closed questions generally are questions that can be answered with a "yes" or a "no". Closed questions are an absolute necessity to the sales conversation. You may ask a closed-ended question such as "How much do you contribute to employee-only coverage?" The employer may reply that he pays 50% of the employee premium and that response is sufficient. Without getting a response such as this one from a closed-ended question, it is impossible to craft a truly meaningful question.

Open-Ended Questions: These questions cannot be answered with a "yes" or "no" and will require that the prospect elaborate on his answer. An example of an open ended question might be: "What influenced your decision to choose the current plan design?" Open-ended questions provide helpful information that can be used to move the conversation forward.

Even though it is important to understand the distinction between open and closed-ended questions, it is a distinction that is not as important as most sales trainers would lead you to believe. It is meaningful questions that provide the roadmap to an objection-free presentation.

A Meaningful Question

Cannot be answered with a "yes" or "no"

Cannot be answered quickly

Makes the prospect think

Affects the emotions

When you ask a prospect what they are hoping to accomplish and without a moment's hesitation they respond that they want to keep their cost down, you have not asked a meaningful question. Not only wasn't the question meaningful but the answer is irrelevant. During the discussion about change I said that people do not know what they do not know and so a quick answer only deals with a superficial issue and not the deeper goals and objectives of the prospect. Benefit brokers tend to focus on superficial issues because it is easy and obvious. Taking cost out of the conversation requires a certain amount of skill. A broker skilled in asking really great questions would reply to cost issue by saying: "For the moment let's assume that I can get exactly what you want at exactly the perfect premium. What is it that you are trying to accomplish by offering benefits in the first place?" On your next appointment try this and I guarantee that the prospect will look at you with a blank expression as they try to digest the question.

Really Bad Questions

Before we look at how to craft a really great question let's take a moment and talk about really bad questions. Here are some common questions used by Benefit Professionals:

How do you handle COBRA currently? The problem with this question is that it either receives an answer that closes the door on a discussion such as, "We have that handled by a third party who does a great job", or it sets the broker up for an adversarial conversation. If the prospect says that they handle it in-house or that the current broker handles it you are forced to seek a weakness to exploit. This puts you in the position of trying to make either the incumbent look bad or the HR department look bad.

What do you like about your current benefits? Once the prospect begins to tell you what they like about their current plan they psychologically begin to wonder why they are talking to you. They are in effect selling themselves on what they currently have.

What isn't your current broker doing for you that you wish he would? There are two problems with this question. First, people do not know what they do not know. It is highly likely that they think that the incumbent is doing a great job, or at least as good a job as they could expect. Second, people do not like to be mean. Unless the incumbent has done a horrible job it is likely that the prospect will respond by saying something nice about the incumbent. Once the prospect says something nice about the incumbent you are finished because once again psychologically they will wonder why they are wasting time with you.

What is your biggest challenge? Like the prior question people do not know what they do not know. The most likely response to this question is that the biggest challenge is the premium increase. This makes the sales conversation about price and it is almost never about price. Every agent in your market will provide the same quotes so the ultimate buying decision will be based on something else. A good friend of mine recently thought that she had the sale in the bag with a group of 150 employees. She presented a partially self-funded quote that, based upon worse-case scenario, would save the company $90,000 over the next 12 months. Despite the large savings, the prospect chose another agent's proposal that saved them less than $20,000. They gave up savings of an additional $70,000. If it was about price they would have moved to my friend.

The primary goal of asking really great questions is to help the prospect identify which of your services will be helpful while avoiding anything that can keep the incumbent in place.

From a sales perspective I define the different types of questions that you will ask by the type of information they will acquire. As an aid in remembering these questions, I suggest that you remember the "**DOOR**" to closing more sales.

The DOOR

The first type of question that you will use is the **D**etail Oriented question. Detail questions are about acquiring necessary facts. For the most part Detail oriented questions are closed-ended questions. They are neither good nor bad but they are necessary. As much as possible you want to get these out of the way early in the sales process because they carry no emotional weight. Details are simply what they are. Some examples of details that you will have to obtain are:

- Number of employees
- Number of covered employees
- Current carrier
- Plan design
- Employer contribution
- Ancillary benefits
- Number of locations
- Voluntary benefits offered

It is a good idea to create a list of all of the facts that you would want to obtain before proceeding.

Objective Oriented Questions are the next category of questions that you will ask. These are questions about the goals and objectives of the prospect. The goal of these questions is to uncover what it is that the prospect wants that he does not currently have. To craft Objective

Oriented Questions you should refer back to your list of benefits. Without knowledge of the benefits you provide, you will only be able to ask superficial questions. Consider these two questions:

1. If I can provide COBRA administration at no cost would that be of value to you?
2. Would it be of value to you if I can help relieve you of regulatory liability under COBRA?

Question number 1 is a common question used by brokers offering this service. It is a completely meaningless question because the instinctive answer is: "It's free? Of course it is of value." But is really doesn't have value because the prospect did not have to think about the response. The second question focuses on a specific outcome of the service being offered and sets up a meaningful conversation. It is highly likely that the prospect will ask for clarification of the regulatory liability issue. Even if the employer did not ask any questions, there is opportunity for the broker to ask a follow-up question (known as a building question) that will make the answer meaningful. The follow-up might be, "Can you tell me a little about why relief from regulatory liability is important to you?" It can be argued that the same follow-up can be used with question #1 but the answer would be about the money or lack thereof.

The Building Question is a special type of Objective Oriented Question designed to make any objective meaningful. Most salespeople suffer from a disease unique to the occupation – Premature Presentation. As soon as the prospect responds that relief from regulatory liability would be beneficial the salesperson launches into a presentation of how he will provide the COBRA administration and with it assume all liability. Unfortunately, just because the prospect agreed that the service would be important does not immediately make it really important. To help the employer think about what this would mean we ask for clarification. The salesperson might use the response above or he might inquire: "What is your understanding about your regulatory liability under COBRA?" The goal here is to help the prospect internalize his answer and connect it to a goal or objective. As the prospect connects an objective with what achieving that objective would mean, his sense of urgency in wanting to take action will increase and moving the conversation forward is much more likely.

Once you have identified a goal and successfully gotten the prospect to elaborate on how achieving that objective would benefit him, it is time to ask the **O**bstacle Question. The obstacle question serves two purposes. First, it forces the prospect to acknowledge that he does not currently have the benefits of achieving the goal. The second, and perhaps more important goal, is that the Obstacle Question gives the prospect the opportunity to connect what he wants with the fact that the incumbent broker has not initiated a discussion of this goal and/or has not done anything about it. Skilled use of the Obstacle Question will eliminate the possibility of the prospect saying: "Let me see if my current broker can do that for me."

An example of an effective sequence of questions follows:

Objective Oriented Question: Would it be of value to you if I can help relieve you of regulatory liability under COBRA?

Building Question: In what way would a release of regulatory liability be of value to you?

Obstacle Question: So, has your current broker ever addressed this issue with you?

The **R** in DOOR stands for Review. The review takes place during the Information Gathering meeting just prior to establishing the next steps. (See Lesson 6).

Homework for Lesson 6

Before reading the list of questions below take a look at your list of services and create five great questions with follow up.

GREAT QUESTIONS

FOR THE BENEFITS BROKER

1. If you chose me as your broker how would you know in six months that I was the best broker that you have ever worked with?
2. When developing your employee benefit program, what goals were you trying to achieve?
   2.1. Why were those goals important to you?
   2.2. How successful have you been?
   2.3. Are those goals still important to you?
   2.4. Can you tell me a little about how you identified those goals?
   2.5. Has your current broker talked with you about your goals?
3. How do you see your benefit program impacting the productivity of your employees?
   3.1. If there were a way that your benefit program could have a positive effect on employee productivity would that be of interest to you?
4. Is it important to you that your employees understand their benefits?
   4.1. How do you see their understanding of their benefits helping your company?
   4.2. How well do you think they understand their benefits today?
   4.3. What has your current broker done to communicate the benefits to employees in a meaningful way?
5. Do you feel that an employee's understanding of the value of the benefits that you provide has an impact on your business?

5.1. If the employees understood the value of the benefits that you provide, what impact would that have on your business?

5.2. In your opinion how much value do the employees place on the benefits that you provide?

5.3. How do you know that that is how they feel?

5.4. In terms of communicating the value of the benefits that you provide, what are you currently doing?

5.5. What do you believe the broker's role should be in communicating the value of the benefits to employees?

5.6. Do you think that it would be helpful to create a survey for employees that would ask about their perception of the value of the benefits that you provide?

5.7. And what has your current broker done to make sure that the employees understand and appreciate the value of the benefits that you provide?

6. If you had an online system that allowed you to input an employee once and it then pre-populated all of the enrollment forms for you, would that be of any value to you?

7. Other than your group health insurance, in what other ways should your benefits broker be able to help you?

8. Would it be important to you to work with an agent that can help you with all aspects of your benefit program?

9. Have you taken a holistic approach to benefit planning or are you working through different agents for different products?

9.1. Would you like one agent who can handle all of your benefits?

9.2. Do the voluntary benefits being offered to your employees duplicate some of the coverage that you are currently providing?

9.3. Is it important to ensure that your employees are not paying for coverage that you already provide?

9.4. How might eliminating any duplication of employee coverage be of value to you?

10. How important is it to you that your benefit broker be able to keep you informed about legislative issues that impact your benefit plan?

10.1. How would that be of value to you?

11. Should your broker be fully knowledgeable in the compliance issues surrounding COBRA, HIPAA, FMLA and Section 125?

12. Is it important to you that your broker periodically review your HIPAA, COBRA, 125 procedures to insure that you are in compliance?

12.1. How does your current broker keep you up to date on compliance issues?

13. Would having someone else handle your COBRA requirements be of value to you?

13.1. In what way would having someone else handling your COBRA duties be of value to you?

13.2. How do you handle COBRA today?

13.3. Has your current broker spoken to you about COBRA, HIPAA, or Section 125 in the last year?

13.4. How do you feel about the lack of communication?

14. Is your primary concern the premium today or is a strategy for cost control more important?

14.1. Other than shopping your plan, what strategy has your current broker suggested to help you get control of costs?

15. What is the most important service that a broker can provide to you?
    15.1. What is it about that service that makes it important to you?
    15.2. How effective has your current broker been in providing that service?
16. How often would you like to have your broker visit with you in person?
    16.1. Tell me a little about what you would want the broker to do during those visits?
    16.2. How often has your current broker visited?
17. If an employee has a claims problem how do you expect that to be handled?
    17.1. Would you want your employees to call the broker if they had a claims problem?
18. How important is it to you that your broker has a staff person that is dedicated to servicing client's needs?
    18.1. Is it important to you that when you call your broker's office you get to speak with a person as opposed to a message machine?
    18.2. If you leave a message for your broker, what is a reasonable time frame for a return telephone call?
19. Other than price, what else will influence your decision in choosing a broker to work with?
20. If we were to identify benchmarks of excellence that you could use to measure and rate my effectiveness, would that be of value to you?
    20.1. Since you can see the value in having benchmarks, is it important to you to actually be able to measure the effectiveness of a broker's service?
    20.2. In what ways would it be helpful to you?

20.3. Has any broker ever worked with you to develop measurements of service effectiveness?

21. What haven't I asked you about that would be important to you?

22. When we get together again I can provide a spreadsheet of all of the quotes of plans from every carrier in the area, or I can bring you the one or two plans that I believe will best help you achieve your goals. Which would you prefer?

23. Is it important to you that your agent has a strong working relationship with the carrier or carriers he recommends?

23.1. How do you see that relationship benefiting you?

23.2. Would you accept a somewhat higher premium for the same benefits if your broker had a stronger relationship with one carrier over another?

24. Do you see the brokers as an extension of your Human Resource department?

24.1. How do you see your agent working with Human Resources?

24.2. How important is it to you that your agent is able to understand the challenges faced by Human Resources?

25. What role do products such as dental insurance, disability income insurance and group term life insurance play in your benefit strategy?

26. How important is the view that your key employees and executives have of the benefits you provide?

26.1. Would a higher level of benefits for your executives be of interest to you?

26.2. In what ways would special benefits for your key employees be of value to you?

The Core Questions

27. What carrier currently has your health plan?
    27.1. Tell me a little about the deductible, coinsurance and co-pays.
    27.2. Are you happy with the available network?
28. Do you currently provide group term life insurance?
    28.1. Do you offer your employees the opportunity to purchase optional term life insurance?
    28.2. Do you offer them the opportunity to purchase optional permanent life insurance?
29. Do you provide either short or long-term disability income?
    29.1. (If yes) Is it employer paid or voluntary?
30. Do you provide your employees a dental plan?
    30.1. (If yes) Is it employer paid or voluntary?
    30.2. (If voluntary) Do you know if it is a usual and customary plan, a discount plan or a schedule of benefits?
31. Do you provide a vision plan?
    31.1. (If yes) Is it employer paid or voluntary?
32. Do you currently have a Section 125 plan?
    32.1. Do you offer the flexible benefit accounts for medical and child care expenses?
33. Do you offer any voluntary benefits?
    33.1. (If yes) What products do you currently offer?
    33.2. What carrier or carriers provides those products?
34. Do you provide a different level of benefit for executives and key employees than for rank and file?
    34.1. Do you provide a disability income carve out for executives?
35. Do you currently provide a retirement plan or a 401K?

36. Do you currently offer a long-term care policy to your employees?
    36.1. (If yes) Is it employer paid or voluntary?
37. How long have you worked with your current agent?
    37.1. How many times have you changed agents over the last five years?
    37.2. Is it your current practice to allow different brokers to quote your plan every year?
38. Does one agent currently handle all of your benefits including the voluntary products?

Homework

Go through the list of questions and choose those apply to your products and services. Make sure to choose a minimum of three high value services that you can provide.

LESSON 7

THE OBJECTION-FREE PRESENTATION

Before reading further take a moment and review your last ten presentations. As you finished your presentation did your any of your prospects make an immediate decision to do business with you or did they ask for a week or two to review the material? Were you able to secure a follow-up appointment or were you left to hope that you were the broker of choice? I ask these questions knowing that at least 90% of you reading this book rarely close a sale immediately after the presentation and 100% of those never ask for a scheduled appointment to review the prospect's concerns.

Before you discount this and think about your extremely high closing ratio you should look at your last ninety days and analyze how many appointments you secured with new prospects. If the only appointments that you go out on are referrals from existing clients (a very good thing) and an average month consists of one or two new prospects, your high conversion ratio is irrelevant. On the other hand if you are securing two to three appointments with new prospects each week and you are converting more than 70% of those into clients you can ignore this section. But if like the great majority of benefit professionals that I speak with you must generate proposals for ten prospects to convert two or three into a client, this chapter can rock your world.

Your first step in developing an objection-free presentation is to be committed to eliminating your current proposal system. Eliminating your current approach to creating a proposal is critical since it is probably based on the industry standard. Your proposal looks something like this:

- Page 1 – About our company / about me
- Page 2 – The carriers that we represent
- Page 3 – Our services and staff
- Page 4 – The Spreadsheet(s)

You might place your pages in a slightly different order but I have little doubt that your current proposal follows this format. What is important about this is that if I am even close you should be asking yourself if every other broker is using a similar format what does that communicate to the prospect? You may have invested more money into your binder, you may have a more professional logo, but at the end of the day you are just like your competitors. Since everyone promises great service, a caring staff, a wide array of services and every broker within 100 miles represents all of the same companies, the only way to convey your difference is to **be** different.

In Lesson 7 you learned about the various questions that open the DOOR to more sales. As you read Lesson 6 on Information Gathering you learned that you have to get the prospect to tell you what it is that he wants and more importantly why he wants it. The goal of this was to raise the prospect's sense of urgency about implementing a change. By asking what the prospect wants and following up with the reasons for wanting it, you help the prospect become emotionally invested in the goals. Decisions are made emotionally but defended logically and it is your job to involve the prospect's emotions. By asking the right questions you are getting the prospect to provide a roadmap to converting him into a client. If you did a good job of identifying what the prospect wants then you know exactly what the proposal must contain.

The Old Proposal

About Our Agency / About Me

If you feel compelled to include information about your organization or about your background, place it at the end of your proposal not at the beginning. Your prospect does not care at all about this information. His decision will not be based on it. Hearing what you have to say about yourself or your agency has nothing to do with what the prospect wants to accomplish. A fairly regular question on this topic is: "But how will a prospect make a decision to work with me if he doesn't know anything about me?" There is no doubt that at some point the prospect may need to know about you, but it is not at the beginning of proposal, it is at the end. It is only after I decide that I think you are the one that I want to go with that I care about how many clients you have or how long you have been in the business.

Remember that the prospect has scheduled time out of a very busy day to meet with you because he wants to learn how you can help him. The single most important thing in your proposal is your solution to my issues. In addition, it is important to put yourself in the shoes of your prospect for a moment. Is there anything negative that you are going to include in this section of the proposal? Absolutely not! So skip this nonsense and get to what the prospect cares about. Finally, remember that all of your competitors have placed this bit of information at the front of the presentation so if you start this way you are communicating the message that you are just like your competitors. Recently I asked readers of my newsletter, "The Monday Marketing Minute", to answer the question about why a prospect should do business with them. Here are a couple of answers:

"I work to solve true needs, offering skillful analysis and targeted solutions."

"I really do CARE about you, I am a great listener, I will listen, probe and re-probe until I can put myself in your shoes."

"I will take the action most advantageous to you, regardless of how it might affect me."

The sad truth is this: there is nothing that you can write about yourself or your agency that can in any meaningful way impact the prospect's decision about which broker to choose.

Carriers Represented

One hundred percent of the proposals that I have seen include this section. They inevitably begin with some version of the following:

"ABC Insurance Agency is proud to be completely independent. This way we can search the market looking for the best products for our clients. As an independent agency we work with all of the following carriers: BC/BS of Anywhere USA, United Healthcare, Aetna, …….. on and on and on."

I understand that your goal is to convey the message that you are an unbiased professional with only the best interests of the client in mind. But, in what way is that different from your competitors? Unless you can offer a proprietary product that your competitors cannot, there is nothing in this section that can create an air of professionalism.

Our Services

Regardless of how many services you can offer the only services that a prospect cares about are those that can help him achieve his objectives. If the prospect believes that Human Resources currently does a good job of managing COBRA, your services in this regard are irrelevant. If you handle additions and deletions of new hires and terminations but the prospect has a person doing that in his office, what is the value of the service? You may remember the discussion in Part One about the difference in Transactional and Transformational Selling. The list of services is very transactional.

If your goal is to provide the prospect a list of services that can be compared with your competitors list, you better be absolutely sure that yours is longer. Lists are only useful when no one else in your area is offering the same services, and even then its value is suspect. The only thing that matters to the prospect about your list of services is which ones will help him achieve his objectives.

The Spreadsheet

During my ten years as a sales coach to benefit professionals I have seen hundreds of proposals. Every agent believes that somehow his/her proposal is different and better than the competition's but the reality is that they are all the same. Some have more graphs and charts and some utilize a more expensive exterior but at the end of the day they all include several pages of spreadsheets.

In the mind of the producer this illustrates the amount of work that was done on behalf of the prospect. But since virtually every agent has the spreadsheet and they all show the same carriers, the message is: "Nothing special here." Ask your next ten prospects (assuming that you actually get that many sales appointments) if they want a spreadsheet showing all of the options or if they would prefer that you show them the solution that you believe is best suited to help them achieve their goals, and I guarantee that eight of them will choose the latter.

The New Proposal and Presentation

Keep the fancy binders or folders with your company's logo and mission statement printed on them because they are invaluable in creating a Brand Identity. But the guts of the proposal are going to be completely rebuilt. If you did a good job during the Information Gathering Stage you were given a Global Positioning System that will guide you to a successful prospect to client conversion without objection. Your new proposal should follow this formula:

Current Situation

The current situation is a review of some very important facts and some not so important. The information contained in this section would include type of company, number of employees, location or locations, benefit management staffing, general management staffing, ownership and current benefits offered. Take a look at the example below:

Current Situation

ABC Company is a North Carolina Corporation specializing in the manufacture of hospital surgical scubs. Currently, the main plant is in Morehead City, North Carolina and the other two locations are Raleigh and Charlotte, North Carolina.

The company has 350 employees. Each location has a Plant Manager and several department managers. ABC Company has a Human Resources department with one V.P. of Human Resources, one Human Resource Manager and three Human Resource assistants with one stationed at each location. The Human Resource Manager has primary day-to-day responsibility of overseeing the administration of benefits.

Current benefits include:

Group Health Plan – Aetna: There is a $1000 annual deductible with a 70/30 co-insurance level and a maximum out-of-pocket of $3000 plus the deductible. Employees presently enjoy a $25 office co-payment and $10/25/50 prescription drug co-payment.

Group Term Life is provided at 1X salary and is through Companion Life

The purpose of this section is simply to reinforce that you understand the company and their current benefits. By including the number of employees, locations and make-up of Human Resources the message that you are sending is: has any other agent bothered to understand how you operate or have they simply gotten quotes? Never forget that differentiation only occurs in the way you manage the conversation, not in what you promise to do. After you have reviewed the current situation, you simply ask if there is anything else about the current situation that the prospect believes that you should know before continuing. When the prospect responds (as he will) that you have pretty well covered everything, you simply ask: "Out of curiosity, do you believe that my having this understanding of your company has any value?" If the prospect says that it does have value, ask for elaboration. Your goal is to solidify in his mind that you have taken a more comprehensive approach to his benefits than anyone else.

Review Goals and Objectives

More than likely it has been two or three weeks since you were last together and there has been a reduction in the sense of urgency. In addition, it is probable that the prospect has forgotten some of what he said was important, so before moving to your presentation you want to refresh his memory. To begin to raise the sense of urgency we review each of the goals. Your next section looks like this:

Goals and Objectives

The company has experienced annual health insurance rate increases of 15% or more with a current renewal increase of 18%. The company has expressed the following goals:

1: Develop a strategy to get control of premiums not just find the lowest current premium

2: Provide a plan design that will act as an incentive to employees to take control of their lifestyle choices

3: Manage employee perceptions – Create a plan design that will not be seen as a reduction in benefits as well as a communication strategy to accomplish this

4: Develop a plan to reduce employee turnover

5: Create benefits that will act to attract and retain executives

---

Your list may be longer but it definitely should not be shorter. You may have identified goals that include:

- Shifting COBRA Liability to a third party
- Developing a strategy to free up premium dollars that can be reallocated to new benefits
- Replacing the current voluntary carrier and agent
- Providing monthly benefit orientation meetings

The important thing here is to only include those objectives that the prospect has explicitly stated were important and was able to elaborate on why they were important. If the prospect did not explicitly state that a HIPAA Compliance Audit was important do not include it!

If you are wondering why this section is so very, very important take a look at your most recent proposal. Where in that proposal is there any mention of the prospect's explicitly stated goals? For the great majority of you reading this, the answer is that there is absolutely no mention of the prospect's goals. When you review the prospect's goals you create a connection between what you are about to present and those goals. After reviewing the goals you simply ask the prospect if you have missed anything or if there are any goals or objectives that the prospect may have that you did not ask about. One hundred percent of the time the prospect is going to tell you that you have covered everything and often he will add the words "very thoroughly." By asking if you have missed anything you will never hear the words: "But how about …" at the conclusion of your presentation.

The Solution

Presenting the solution is the trickiest part of the presentation from the standpoint of the written proposal. There are a couple of things that you want to avoid in your solution. First, avoid any use of jargon such as Health Savings Accounts, HRA or self-funding. Since these terms tend to carry emotional baggage, it is best to talk in terms of plan design instead. If you are going to be presenting a radical departure from the current plan design, you may want to consider presenting it first from the standpoint of the employee. Let us assume that you are moving this company from the current $1000 deductible with co-payments for both doctor's visits as well as prescription drugs to a $5000 high deductible health plan with no office visit copayments but retaining a prescription drug benefit. To fill the gaps in this plan you are inserting a limited medical benefit plan that pays a $2500 lump sum benefit upon the first hospital admission, $1250 for outpatient diagnostic tests and reimburses the employee up to $75 for each doctor visit. This plan design reduces the employer's monthly cost per employee from $450 (after the rate increase) to $375. Prior to the rate increase, the employer's cost was $395.00 so the new plan reduces his per employee cost by $240 annually.

In presenting this plan I would begin with the goal of controlling costs rather than the plan design. Immediately following the cost savings and control aspect I would move to the plan as the employee will have it explained. It is only after I get conceptual buy-in that I would explain the mechanics of the actual plan design. If you begin by explaining the component parts of the new plan you invite objections. This part of the proposal would look like this:

Goal # 1 – Get Control of Costs

The recommended plan design will reduce the per employee premium by $900 annually. Multiplied by the current 35 employees ABC Company will save $31,500 this year.

It is our recommendation that ABC establish a separate account to be used to accumulate these funds for use in off-setting future design changes.

New Plan Design from the Employee Perspective
Current plan design requires that employees pay the first $1000 of any hospital admission or outpatient diagnostic testing. Under the new plan the first $2500 of a hospital admission is paid at 100%. The employee will be responsible for the next $2500. Currently any diagnostic tests such as an MRI are subject to the $1000 deductible. Under the recommended plan design any diagnostic tests such as an MRI are paid at 100% on the first $1250. An insured is responsible for amounts above the $1250. Once the employee has total combined expenses of $5000 for either in-patient or diagnostic testing, the plan will pay the balance at 80% with a maximum out of pocket of $2000. This is the same as the current plan.

Doctor visit copayments - Currently the employee must pay a $35 co-payment per visit. Under the new plan the employee will have the first $75 of the office visit paid at 100%. This should result in no out-of-pocket cost to the employee.

The recommended plan design retains the current prescription drug benefit in its current form.
Total Out-of-Pocket Costs

Current plan: $3000 including the deductible but no first dollar coverage

Recommended Plan: $4500 (in-patient) / $5750 (out-patient). This is offset by the fact that most outpatient diagnostic tests such as the MRI are covered at 100% on the first $1250. It is highly likely that the employee will incur less out-of-pocket expense under this plan design.

Goal # 2 – Manage Employee Perceptions

Step 1 – Employee group meetings where the new plan can be explained with emphasis on first dollar coverage features.

Step 2 – We recommend that ABC set aside up to $25/month per employee in a Medical Expense Reimbursement

The proposal would continue in this fashion through each of the employer's goals. Only after identifying each goal and linking it to the solution would I ask for conceptual agreement on the proposal.

Conceptual Agreement

Throughout this chapter I have been referring to the idea of obtaining conceptual agreement before continuing the presentation and so it makes sense to spend some time defining this term. Most Benefit Professionals never obtain conceptual agreement before presenting their proposal. Instead they simply launch into a review of the current plan and then walk the prospect through the spreadsheet analyzing the different plans and identifying their recommendation. Their focus is on the plan and the premium and not on ideas and strategies which are the key elements of the Compelling Conversation™. Conceptual agreement can only be obtained where there is a discussion of objectives and the strategies to achieve them.

To obtain conceptual agreement you must first establish a number of goals that the prospect wants to achieve other than just a reduced premium. If you are presenting a High Deductible Health Plan such as a Health Savings Account, talking about the theory of giving employees the incentive to manage their health care is not a foundation for obtaining conceptual agreement. Asking the employer whether it is important to provide financial incentives to employees in order to motivate them to take personal responsibility for their healthcare decisions and then following up with a request for elaboration does provide the foundation for conceptual agreement. Presenting a carriers proposal and asking for feedback is not conceptual agreement. Describing the HSA as it would be presented to the employees and then asking the prospect whether he believes that this approach will help achieve a specific goal is obtaining conceptual agreement.

The difference between presenting a strategy and presenting the actual plan design is huge and critical to an objection-free presentation. This can best be seen by relating the story of two benefit professionals operating in Fayetteville, North Carolina. In 2004 Broker # 1 routinely sold a $5000 deductible health plan with a GAP product to all of his groups. His approach was to use this combination as a part of a long-term strategy that would provide premium control to the employer. When I met with Broker # 2 about this concept his response was: "Mel, you have to understand that businesses in Fayetteville will never buy into this plan." He had attempted this approach but found that his prospects seemed to always ask if they could buy the high deductible plan without the GAP plan. This result occurred because he simply presented the high deductible health plan and then presented the GAP plan rather than presenting a cohesive strategy first. Broker # 1, a consummate salesperson, always presented the composite picture and obtained agreement that this was a good idea before presenting the component parts.

Obtaining conceptual agreement goes beyond the plan design and strategy. It includes getting agreement on getting referrals if certain benchmarks are met, on becoming the sole source of all insurance products related to employee benefits as well as all of your other goals for this prospect. If you obtain agreement that your strategy is sound and will help achieve the identified outcomes, there is nothing to object to later. A prospect may object to a health reimbursement arrangement because of some preconceived ideas, but there is nothing to object to if you present the same plan as a strategy explicitly linked to the achievement of a specific goal.

Closing the Sale

Once you have obtained conceptual agreement on your strategy you simply state that, with this in mind, you would like to show them how all of the parts work together. Now is the time to walk the prospect through the component pieces of your strategy. If you are going to present a radical departure from the status quo as was the case with Broker # 1 above (the $5000 deductible coupled with a GAP plan) you will want to preface the presentation with a reminder that they agreed to the overall strategy. As you walk the prospect through the proposal periodically relate a feature to a benefit and advantage. This will help keep the prospect's eyes on the outcomes rather than getting bogged down in the minutia.

The Summary Recap

Once you have walked the prospect through the entire presentation it is time to do a summary review. The approach that most salespeople take can be seen in the following:

"Ms. Prospect, before we conclude let me just review what I am presenting. The plan that I have presented will help you reduce your premium by moving from a $1000 deductible to a $5000 deductible. To insure that the employees do not revolt we will include a GAP plan underwritten by ABC Insurance Company. To offset the elimination of the office visit copayments this plan will provide a direct reimbursement of up to $75 per doctor office visit."

The problem with this approach is that it does nothing to verify that the prospect understood the value of your proposal. Even if you ask the prospect if there are any questions you will have no sense of whether the prospect has bought into your proposal or not.

Rather than you providing the summary review you want to ask your prospect to do the review. This is a very different approach to the closing but extremely effective. The set-up for this request is logical and will result in complete buy-in on the part of the prospect. To get your prospect to do the summary you simply say the following:

"Ms. Prospect, have you ever had a situation where what you believed that someone had promised and what that person believed was not exactly the same thing?"

I guarantee that one hundred percent of the time the response will be affirmative. There is no doubt in my mind that you have personally had this happen because we all experience this. Once you obtain an affirmative response you continue:

"Well as I indicated earlier, I really want to be the best benefit professional that you have ever worked with. To accomplish that, it is important to me that what you believe I am promising, and what I think that I am promising, are the same things. With that in mind, would you mind sharing with me your understanding of what I am promising to do and how you see it helping you and your company?"

As surprising as this is going to sound your prospect will smile and gladly oblige. Talk about differentiation! No other salesperson has ever asked the prospect to do the summary recap. More importantly the prospect will instantly see the value of this approach. Only a benefit professional with impeccable integrity would want to ensure that there was no misunderstanding before moving forward with the relationship. Periodically throughout the recap ask for some elaboration. For example, the prospect might say that the program that you are presenting includes placing $25 monthly into a medical reimbursement account for employees to use to offset some out-o-pocket expenses. You would simply ask the prospect to share with you the ways that he sees this helping to achieve his goals. You do not want to ask for elaboration on every point but by doing so in a judicious manner, you facilitate the internalization of your strategy.

After the prospect completes the summary recap you will simply ask if he has any questions or concerns that have not been addressed by the proposal. It would be a highly unusual circumstance where the prospect has a question or concern at this point. This is followed by a question about any goals that have not been addressed by this strategy, and once again, there should be no other goals. The only thing left to do at this juncture is to ask for the sale. There are two approaches to asking for the sale and you can work with the one that is most comfortable to you. The first approach is to simply look the prospect in the eyes and ask: "So based on everything that you have just said; what should the next step be?" If you have involved all decision-makers, the prospect cannot in good conscience say that he needs to think about it. If you are somewhat more aggressive you may choose to use the assumed close. The assumed close would sound like this: "So based on everything that you just said when should we schedule the enrollment to begin?" Each approach has its positive and negative points but the one that you choose should be comfortable for your style. I generally choose the former because I like to let prospects buy rather than feel sold. It suits my personality better. That said, I know that many of my clients use the assumed close very effectively and find that there is less chance of delay in getting a decision.

Conclusion

The Compelling Conversation™ approach to presenting will require a retooling of your current proposal system. Rather than information about you and your agency followed by a set of spreadsheets your new proposal will be very prospect centered. You will focus on specific, explicitly stated goals and the strategies that will help achieve them. Before getting to actual plan designs you will review your strategy and discuss the plan from the perspective of the employees. Then you obtain conceptual agreement that the proposed strategy will indeed achieve the desired goals. Finally, you will ask the prospect to do a summary review of what it is that you are proposing and how the prospect sees that contributing to the achievement of stated goals. All that is left is to ask for the sale.

LESSON 8

THE COMPETITOR-PROOF ACCOUNT

Before moving on to the presentation phase of the sales process we have to spend some time on the subject of providing awesome service. There is unanimous agreement that client retention is a function of how good your after-the-sale service is. And I have never met a benefit professional that felt that he did a poor job at servicing his accounts. At every program that I do I ask benefit professionals what they mean by great service and the answers are always the same. One hundred percent of the time the responses that I get include:

1. My clients have unlimited access to me day or night
2. I return calls as soon as possible
3. My clients know that they should call my office when there is a claims or billing problem and we will handle it
4. We handle the additions and deletions
5. We do a good job of shopping their plans every year
6. We provide an online system where employees can access their benefits
7. We provide HR an online system where they can reconcile their bills with one click
8. We provide our clients an online HR library
9. We handle the COBRA for our clients
10. The employees call us instead of going to HR

While each of these may have value, there is absolutely no connection between these services and great service.

Several months ago I received a call from a broker in Michigan that offered many of the above services. His problem was that despite all of the services that he provided he had just lost two accounts to an agent of record letter. He was absolutely befuddled because he had these accounts for several years and had never had a complaint from either of them. But this is not an isolated event. Earlier this week I had lunch with a broker in North Carolina who shared a similar story. He had worked with a client for more than three years and had saved them over $70,000 in health insurance premiums the year that he took over as their broker. Despite that the Vice President of Human Resources put the dental plan out for quote after receiving a 3% rate increase, which was the first increase in two years. With 24/7 access to this broker they moved the dental plan to save less than 5% in annual premium.

So, here is the million dollar question: If your service is so great why do you ever lose an account?

The Million Dollar Question

If your service is so great, why do you ever lose an account?

Occasionally a broker will tell me that he rarely loses a client and many of his clients have been with him with three, five, ten years or longer and that must say something about his service. The length of time that a client is with you may say something about your service but more often than not it simply means that the client does not think that any broker will do anything differently – and that is not synonymous with great service. Have you ever actually asked a client what they thought of your service in a way that would provide a meaningful answer? Undoubtedly you have asked the following question at renewal: "So is there anything that I am not doing that you wished that I would?" You may have asked one of the variations of this question such as:

"You have been my client for the past _ years, can you tell me how you feel that I am doing?"

"Over the past year how would you rate my service?"

"Is there anything that you are unhappy with as it pertains to the job that I am doing for you?"

By themselves the answers that you get from these inane questions are irrelevant. Unless there is something that you did that angered a client the easy answer is that you are doing a fine job. It is only when you ask a follow-up question that you begin to learn how meaningless this really is. Kimberly, a coaching client of mine, had the following dialogue with a client at renewal:

Kimberly: You have been my client for more than five years now so can I ask you to tell me how you feel about my service?
Client: Kimberly, you do a great job.
Kimberly: Is there something specific that I do?
Client: I just think that you do a great job.
Kimberly: If you were to change brokers, what would a new broker have to do so that you would think that broker was the best broker that you ever worked with?
Client: Well, all of the things that you do for us Kimberly.

Kimberly: That's great but what exactly would you want a new broker to do if you didn't have me? Assume that I never existed, what services specifically would you want?

There are a couple of very important points about this dialogue. First, the fact that a client cannot think of specific services tells you that this is an account that can be gotten by another broker who can present a new service that they do not currently have. Since there is nothing that this client can state is an important service means that nothing is important. They may really like Kimberly but there is nothing that they can use to measure her by. There are no benchmarks of excellence. But more importantly Kimberly has no idea whether she is working hard enough to keep this account or working harder than she needs to, which may be the more valuable information. As Kimberly would learn after further dialogue she was providing a service that she thought was important but that the employer didn't care about. That service was Kimberly's monthly visit to meet with new hires. Kimberly thought that this was an extremely meaningful service but after a lengthy discussion where she finally got the prospect to explicitly state services that were important, this one was never discussed. Finally Kimberly asked the prospect about these monthly visits and was told that they were unnecessary because the HR assistant always met with and enrolled new hires in the benefits and made sure to answer any questions. They certainly appreciated Kimberly's visits but if she wanted to stop them that would be perfectly alright with them. Kimberly then asked how they felt about her visiting on a quarterly basis so that she could be available to any employee that had a question or a problem. The Human Resource Director told her that would be great and probably would have more value to the employees.

I share Kimberly's story because it is illustrative of the approach that most Benefit Professionals take to service. They promise the moon in the hopes that they can "wow" the client into submission and cut off any competitors. Unfortunately this generally does not have the intended effect of making a client competitor-proof. And it certainly does not create in the words of Ken Blanchard "Raving Fans." That brings me to one final point before moving on to the formula for creating the competitor-proof account and that deals with referrals. Whenever I talk about this I get at least one broker that tells me that he works exclusively on referral because his clients are always recommending him to others. Before moving on we need to make a major distinction between a real referral from a "Raving Fan" and the situation where your client is nothing more than a "Yellow Page" directory for another business person.

To distinguish between the two you need to ask one question about the origin of the referral. That question is: "Did the prospect just get a rate increase and was asking friends who they used for benefits (yellow page directory) or did your client tell this person how great you were without any prompting?" More often than not it is the former situation that generates the referral. But the "Raving Fan" may be having lunch with a business person and simply says without prompting that they have an incredible agent working for them and that if their associate ever wants service that is extraordinary, they should call you. The difference between these two types of referrals is enormous but to generate a "Raving Fan" requires that your clients be able to identify what it is that you actually do for them. It is more than being told that you do a great job, it is being told the specific tasks that you do that they appreciate.

Making Service Meaningful

Great after-the-sale service is an incredibly rare event in the group benefits arena. Everyone thinks that they provide really great service but no one really knows what that means. Whenever I attend a meeting of a State Association of Health Underwriters, I will ask brokers the "why should I do business with you" question. Ninety-five percent of the time the response is "because I provide great service." When I ask what that means I get the deer in the headlights look. So how do I define great service? Great service is whatever the client says it is!

Great Service

Whatever the client says it is!

Rather than launching into a litany of all the wonderful things that you can do, the goal is to let the prospect tell you what it is that they want from you. My favorite transition from rapport building (small talk) to the sales conversation is this:

"Ms. Prospect, I know that over the years you have probably met with a lot of brokers haven't you?"

"And every one of them has come in here and told all about themselves and their agency and told you all of the wonderful things that they were going to do for you, didn't they?"

"Well, I do not operate that way. I am not going to tell you about all of the services that I can provide and all of the carriers that I do business with because the only thing that matters to me is learning what matters to you. So with that in mind, if you were to choose to work with me, how would you know in six months that I was the best broker that you have ever worked with? What is that I would have to do?"

Most brokers have a very hard time giving up the "let me tell you about myself" opening. They think that somehow what they are going to say is different from the competition. Unfortunately for you, your prospect does not care about any of that until they decide that you are the broker of choice. The beauty of this opening is that it immediately differentiates you from everyone else. More importantly, most prospects will be unable to answer this question which provides the opportunity to ask really great questions based on your services to uncover what is important and why. If the prospect actually knows what they want it gives you the opportunity to decide if you can live up to their expectations or not. If you believe that what they are asking for is unreasonable say so, and move on to another client. Just because you can get the case does not mean that you should. There are two goals for this approach. First, you want to manage expectations and second, you want to establish benchmarks of excellence so that your client can provide meaningful feedback at a later date.

Managing Expectations

Whether you want to admit this or not the sad truth of benefit sales is that most brokers over-promise and under-deliver. You cannot have 60, 70 or more accounts and provide the promised level of service. Even if you do everything that you promise it will be underwhelming. The reason is that you promise so much that it is all that you can do meet expectations and meeting expectations does not create the "WOW" factor. It is only when you exceed expectations that the client is truly impressed. Let us look at an example.

Scenario A

Assume that you promise a client that you will visit monthly and meet with new hires to answer questions and explain the benefits. If you show up monthly what have you done? You have met expectations.

Meeting expectations is what is expected of you. It does nothing to make you stand out. But what if instead of promising everything that you can do, you were able to get the prospect to tell you what was important? Staying with the example of regular visits to a client, what would happen if you had the following exchange:

Broker: Ms. Prospect, is it important to you to have your broker visit on a regular basis?

Prospect: Yes, it is important to me that the broker come by more often than at renewal.

Broker: So, if you were to choose to work with me, how often would you like me to stop by? Is once a month what you are expecting or would quarterly be sufficient?

Prospect: Quarterly should work.

Broker: And what do you hope to have accomplished during these quarterly visits?

Prospect: Just be available for a couple of hours to answer any employee questions or solve their problems.

Now look at Scenario B:

Scenario B

Assume that you promise a client that you will visit quarterly to meet with new hires to answer questions and explain the benefits. If you show up monthly and say that you just wanted to check in and see if anyone needed you, what have you done?

You have now exceeded expectations!

Which scenario has a bigger "WOW" factor? I hope that you chose Scenario B as the bigger "WOW". Brokers tend to follow Scenario A out of fear that someone else will promise more than they do and thus will get the case. The truth is that once you have the conversation where the prospect says that quarterly is what is important it will not matter if another broker promises weekly visits.

By allowing the prospect to tell you what it is that he wants you effectively manage your workload because the prospect will always want less in the way of service than you were going to promise. You will want to follow this formula until you have identified three or four key expectations of the prospect. Remember that this is being done during the Information Gathering phase so it is imperative that you do not promise to deliver any of the requested services. Many brokers suffer from Premature Presentation. This is where a prospect says that they want monthly visits and the broker's mouth goes into gear and says: "If you work with me, I promise to provide monthly visits. In fact I will come by every two weeks." During Information Gathering you never state what you are going to do.

Establishing Benchmarks of Excellence

Once you have identified the three of four key expectations you want to establish a system of review. To do this you simply say the following:

Broker: "Ms. Prospect, just to review. Your expectations of a great broker are the following: quarterly on-site visits with employees, COBRA Administration services, and the ability to provide you with single-source billing for all of the benefits that you offer. Is that correct?"

Prospect: That's correct.
Broker: So if I deliver on these services, then in your eyes, I would be the best broker that you have ever worked with. Am I understanding you correctly?
Prospect: I guess so.
Broker: Great. So here are my expectations of you should I become your broker. First, I want you to agree that in three months and again in six months we will meet and review each if these expectations. I need you to promise that you will be absolutely honest and

tell me how I am doing in each of these areas. Will you agree to that?

Prospect: Sure, that sounds like a great idea.

Broker: So if I meet or exceed your expectations and I qualify as the best broker that you have ever worked with, I want your agreement that I get to handle all of your benefit needs including retirement, voluntary, executive and business life insurance. Is that doable?

You will definitely want to do a three and six month benchmark review. From the perspective of your new client this will be a new and valuable experience. No other broker has ever requested this, let alone provided specific benchmarks that can be used to measure the effectiveness of the servicing broker. Assuming that you do a good job, the review will solidify your place with that client. The review is also the ideal time to ask for referrals. If you want to create a "Raving Fan" this is it! Your new clients will not wait to be asked by another person for the name of a great broker. Instead they will readily tell their associates about the broker that actually asks to me reviewed. You will indeed be competitor-proof.

As I indicated in the lesson on Information Gathering, you close the appointment by reviewing the goals of the prospect and then establish a scheduled next step. This is where you will once more review the criteria for achieving great broker status. When you return with your presentation you will once more review the criteria as well as other important objectives before moving into the actual presentation.

LESSON 9

CROSS-SELLING

This lesson is for those benefit professionals that want to increase their income by 50% or more in the next twelve months without increasing the number of clients being serviced. Now you might be thinking that everyone would want to do that but the truth is that the most overlooked income producing opportunity is within your current book of clients. Group benefit producers tend to be so focused on securing the next opportunity to quote a health plan that they never spend any time looking for the sales opportunities within their client base. Even more astounding to me is the number of agents who have no idea what other benefits exist within their clients. Worse yet are those benefit producers who believe that if a client had an interest in wellness, voluntary benefits or other line of coverage, the client would ask about it.

As a general agent calling on brokers about voluntary benefits and/or ancillary benefits the number one response is always: "I will give you a call if one of my clients asks me about that." Unfortunately most clients will move forward with another agent before calling you because they do not see you as a "Benefit Consultant". In the eyes of your clients you are the group health agent and do not market those other products. I know that at some point in your relationship you told the client that you sell voluntary benefits, ancillary benefits, executive benefits and wellness but they really weren't listening so they don't think of you. If you think that you are different, I would ask you this question: "When was the last time you initiated a conversation about a product that was not already in place with your clients?" I am not referring to telling the prospect at renewal that you can sell these other products. I am asking if you have ever asked a client: "Ms. Prospect, I would like to talk with you about the value of adding _____."

Marc is one of my newer coaching clients who surveyed his clients to identify potential sales opportunities. As it turned out one of his larger clients (250 employees) allowed their employees to purchase voluntary benefits from another agent. After reviewing what was offered Marc discovered that employees were spending $200,000 in voluntary premiums. He ultimately received permission to replace the existing coverage and generated more than $100,000 in new, first year commissions. More importantly he provided comparable coverage and saved the employees a significant amount of money. The employees had a better understanding of how these voluntary benefits worked in conjunction with their core benefits and he helped several employees eliminate duplication of coverage.

One of my clients in Virginia discovered that many of clients were open to a discussion of executive disability income coverage as a supplement to the basic long term disability income plan in place. This became a comfortable secondary market and a natural fit with his approach to the benefit marketplace. Every time he quoted both long and short term disability he began to pay attention to the amount of executive compensation that was covered by the base plan. He soon discovered that not only was this a great cross-selling opportunity, but it was also a great back door approach to new business.

When to Initiate the Cross-Selling Conversation

In my mind there are three opportunities for initiating this conversation. The first opportunity occurs at the point of initial sale, the second opportunity is during the annual renewal and the third opportunity is anytime during the year.

In Lesson 2 on Informational Gathering I stressed the importance of learning about all of the benefits beyond the usual core benefits that are in place. From this initial fact finding you can identify where a cross selling opportunity might exist. If for example I identified that a particular prospect did not currently provide a short term disability income plan I would formulate my strategy around that benefit. On the other hand if the prospect currently offered voluntary benefits through an agent other than the group health incumbent that would be my focus. The actual cross-selling does not take place as part of the actual proposal presentation. Instead it occurs after the prospect has made a decision to go or not go with you as the new agent. This is known as the "Oh by the way" strategy and goes like this:

Step 1: Schedule an enrollment strategy meeting

Prospect: Joe, we decided to go with you on the group benefits.

Agent: That's great! What I would like to do is schedule some time for us to meet and discuss the enrollment strategy that will best help us achieve your benefit objectives.

Prospect: That sounds like a great plan.

Step 2: The enrollment meeting discussion

Agent: One of your goals was to ensure that your employees have a good understanding and appreciation of the benefits that you provide. Is that still an important goal for you?

Prospect: Absolutely! That is critical to me.

Agent: So here is what I propose – let's schedule small group meetings where I can explain all of the benefits that you provide and answer any questions. Then I can walk the group through the enrollment process. How does that sound so far?

Prospect: That actually makes sense to me.

Agent: Great!   One more thing: I noticed when we were reviewing your benefits that you have not made any provision of sick leave policies or disability income. For just $X monthly you can add a short term disability income benefit that would provide employees enough income replacement to cover their COBRA premium should they be unable to work for up to six months. This would be perceived as a high value benefit even though your cost would be minimal. If employees want to increase their coverage they can add to it and pay the difference. Can you see any reason not to move forward with this strategy?

In my experience using a voluntary benefit with this close tends to be more effective than using an employer paid benefit but both approaches will have success. Of course the easiest route to success is to replace an existing product line. If there are existing lines of coverage not with the incumbent it is very likely that the prospect will not object to either allowing you to replace the existing coverage or to becoming the agent of record.

The second cross-selling opportunity occurs at the renewal. The only difference between cross-selling at point of sale and at renewal is that you must bring it up prior to creating a proposal. If there is a replacement opportunity available that is the route of least resistance. If you are going to initiate a new sale conversation I suggest that you make skillful use of your questions to identify what your client wants to achieve and then position your product suggestion in terms of that goal.

The third and most effective cross-selling opportunity is a mid-year cross-selling conversation. Within the current book of business there are numerous sales opportunities just waiting to be identified. These opportunities may include:

- ✓ Voluntary benefits
- ✓ Executive carve out disability income
- ✓ Long Term Care
- ✓ Supplemental Executive Retirement Plans
- ✓ Retirement Plans including the 401K
- ✓ Group disability income – both long and short term
- ✓ Dental Plans – both voluntary and employer-paid
- ✓ Wellness Benefits

Too many insurance agents selling in the group market are less about being the complete benefit professional and more about simply selling the group health plan without identifying other plans in place.

To identify potential sales opportunities have a team member (or yourself) call every client with a minimum of 10 employees. You will want to talk with your usual contact even if he/she is not the decision-maker since this is simply about identifying what is or is not currently in place.

Step 1 - Telephone Script

Hello _____ this is _____ with (Name of agent or agency).

First I want to thank you for giving us the opportunity to be of service to you and your employees.

Second, in an attempt to provide the best possible service to our benefit clients we are updating our records so do you have a few minutes to answer a few quick questions?

Great! According to my records we currently handle your (list the benefits you handle).

Do you currently provide any other employer-paid benefits such as (LTD, STD, Dental or Retirement)?

And do you offer your employees the opportunity to purchase voluntary benefits such as cancer insurance or accident insurance?

Finally do you currently offer your key executives any special benefits such as disability income or long term care?

Thanks for your time and if there is ever anything that we can do for you please do not hesitate to call.

Step 2 – Send a handwritten Thank You Note

Dear Ms. HR Professional

Thank you so much for taking the time to talk with me earlier today. The information that you shared will help us better serve you, our client.

If there is anything that we can to do to assist you in better managing your benefits please do not hesitate to call us.

Sincerely

Joe
Joe Agent
(444) 555-7788

Step 3 – Evaluate For Potential

A. Look for existing benefits
1. Existing benefits that are with another agent present the easiest opportunities since this sale does not require a decision to spend new dollars. The most common opportunities in this category will be voluntary benefits and ancillary benefits.
B. Look for Opportunities with Products Your Are Comfortable With
1. You may be more comfortable opening a conversation about the need for disability income or dental than about Long Term Care or Executive Benefits. By beginning with those clients that do not currently have those benefits you will increase the possibility of a positive outcome.
C. Categorize Remaining Clients by Profit Potential
1. It is now time to begin to work your remaining clients based on profit potential. This may require that you get out of your comfort zone and stretch yourself. You may have to learn about new product lines and/or create strategic relationships with other brokers

Step 4 – Contact Clients

It is now time to contact existing clients and ask for the chance to meet with them about an idea that can help them accomplish some goal.

Some suggestions:

Voluntary Benefits

Ms. Client this is _____ . Recently your spoke with Jane Smith and shared some information about existing benefits. As I was reviewing that information I noticed that you currently offer your employees voluntary cancer and accident insurance. The reason for my call this morning is that we are finding that as the cost of other benefits rise many of our clients have started to review these voluntary benefits in much the same way that they review their health plans. That is that they want to make sure that they offering the best plans to their employees at the lowest possible premiums. If I can provide equal or better benefits to your employees and save them money in premium dollars would you be open to meeting with me for 15 minutes?

Dental Insurance

Ms. Client this is _____ . Recently your spoke with Jane Smith and shared some information about existing benefits. As I was reviewing that information I noticed that you currently provide your employees a dental insurance plan. We have a new design in dental insurance that increases employee appreciation of the benefit and lowers premium. Would you be interested in learning more about the chance to lower premiums and improve employee appreciation?

Disability Income

Ms. Client this is _____ . Recently you spoke with Jane Smith and shared some information about existing benefits. As I was reviewing that information I noticed that you do not currently offer your employees a disability income insurance plan. After health insurance, this is one of the most valuable benefits that you can offer your employees and the one that can actually help your company's bottom line. I have a couple of ideas that can help you provide this benefit at little or even no cost to your company. Would you be willing to spend 10 minutes with me to further discuss this idea?

ARTICLE LIBRARY

A COMPILATION OF SALES ARTICLES

The Snail Mail Advantage

Here is a novel thought: stop using email as your communication tool of choice. I am not suggesting that you totally stop using email since there are instances where it is appropriate. If you are working on a proposal and need your prospect to send you some information an email should suffice. If you need a form signed an email will work. But when it comes to marketing and relationship building email is completely useless.

Since October I have asked hundreds of insurance agents the following question:

"Do you routinely send a handwritten thank you note to every prospect that has met with you?"

The results of my informal survey showed that 97% of the agents were sending an email thank you note to their prospects. Now consider this: imagine that two people are competing for your business and very much like the group health insurance market, both have the same products and the same rates. One competitor sends you an email thank you note and the other sends you a handwritten note by snail mail. Which one will have the competitive edge? Several of the agents that I have spoken with stated that they sent e-cards, not just simple email. My response is that that is simply so 1995! The sad truth is that everyone is inundated with emails every day. Anything rated as less than important but not urgent is very quickly relegated to the trash bin and that includes e-thank you cards. That means that your e-card will barely register before it is simply deleted.

I actually encourage my sales coaching clients to send a thank you card immediately after scheduling an appointment with a prospect. The note is very simple:

"I just wanted to thank you in advance for taking the time out of your schedule to meet with me next Tuesday, March 5 at 9AM. Prior to that meeting please give some thought to your benefit goals."

Recently one of my clients entered a prospect's office and saw his pre-thank you card on the prospect's desk. Before the meeting began the prospect actually commented on how much she appreciated the card. She explained that she rarely received a handwritten note after an appointment and never before an appointment. The fact that my client showed an appreciation for her time made a real impact on her impression of him.

Direct Mail and Lead Generation

In the January 12, 2010 issue of the Wall Street Journal Online there was a great article titled: "Firms Hold Fast to Snail Mail Marketing." The article gives a number of examples of firms that shifted their marketing budgets to email marketing and actually saw their revenue drop considerably. The writer uses as an example the experience of Alicia Settle, the owner of a small business. Since she was spending $20,000 annually on direct mail she thought that the savings in time and money plus the increased exposure due to the increased numbers of potential customers that can be touched by email marketing would be huge. The result of her switch to email marketing was a 25% reduction in orders from the same period a year earlier. By switching back to snail mail using postcard marketing she increased her sales enough to completely recoup her lost revenue from the email marketing switch.

One of the most important aspects of Ms. Settle's direct mail campaign is the fact that she used postcard marketing. Postcards have the advantage of getting read as opposed to the more traditional form letter. The challenge with form letters is getting the envelope opened. While there are a number of techniques that will get form letters opened, the real question is why even bother when postcards easily grab attention of the prospect? Of course there is another very important consideration and that is the fact that postcards require less postage than letters and are cheaper overall to create.

In my own marketing I use postcards as part of a drip mail campaign. Most recently I began to market an innovative voluntary benefit program built around employee health promotion. To warm up my calls I send two different cards to the presidents of companies with 100 to 499 employees. The postcards are separated by two days so that they will make more of an impression and will be easily remembered when I call to follow-up. Those prospects that do not grant me an appointment are then placed in my 12 month wellness drip mail campaign. Each month my prospects receive a postcard with a different wellness message tied to obscure celebrations. An example of one of these obscure celebrations is in April which is both National Stress Awareness Month and National Humor Month. I guess the message in April is to reduce stress with humor!

By using direct mail postcards you will have a distinct advantage since most of your competitors are trying to focus on online marketing. Most of your prospects get very little junk mail anymore and will pay attention to a simple postcard message. That said it is important to recognize that you cannot simply send fifty postcards and expect to get an avalanche of telephone inquiries. In fact you are likely to get not one single call after that mailing. Sales success requires consistency of action and time. I send my mailings to 10 new prospects every single week. I then follow up with telephone calls the following week. I leave voice messages at least twice and then send a greeting card with a $5 Starbucks Gift card enclosed and a note. Do I get appointments? You bet! Do I get a lot of appointments? I do not need a lot of appointments. I do need a few very high quality appointments and that is my goal.

A Simple System

There is a revolutionary new technology that makes the sending of postcards, greeting cards and multi-panel cards as simple as sending an email. And although I am using technology, the cards are written in my handwriting and have an actual stamp on them. This system makes sending drip campaigns incredibly simple and requires a minimal time investment. Still, you do have to be committed to taking the steps necessary to generate a meaningful return.

In addition to the available technology you will also need a good sales contact management system. I personally use zoho.com. It is inexpensive and allows me to see the results of my various sales campaigns. If you want to know what is working and what is not working you need to be able to track everything that you are doing. Zoho provides great graphics that allow you to instantly see how you are doing. Combine a great contact manager with great mail technology and you have the makings of amazing sales results.

Four Words That Increase Per Group Revenue

I want to begin by sharing a couple of success stories because they illustrate the power of these four words. A State Farm Agent in Maryland triples her life sales in March January and has sold more life insurance in the first quarter than in all of 2009. A benefit professional in North Carolina just added voluntary life to one of his accounts by using these words for the first time. Another benefit professional increased his per-group revenue by 60% in 2009 using these four words. So what are these four words?

"Oh, by the way"

This is an amazingly simple technique that can be used to sell new products and services to both new and existing clients. To understand how to use this technique let me set the stage. If you are like most of the benefit professionals that I talk with it is extremely rare that you close the sale immediately following your presentation. In most cases the presentation appointment ends with the prospect asking for some time to review your proposal before making a decision. One or two weeks later the prospect informs you that he has chosen to move forward with you. Rather than simply scheduling the enrollment, ask for an appointment to discuss the best strategy to enroll the group and help the employer achieve his objectives. Then follow these steps:

1: Review the employer's goals that relate to improving employee morale, productivity or improvement in retention of high quality employees.

2: Suggest small group meetings to enhance employee understanding of the new benefits.

3: Ask for agreement that this strategy is what would work best in achieving the employer's goals.

4: Then add the "Oh, by the way"

    a. "Oh, by the way, while enrolling your employees in the group health plan I will also give them a chance to participate in some voluntary life insurance. Do you see any problem with that?"

    b. "Oh, by the way, during the enrollment I would like to offer your key executives the opportunity to add long term care insurance to their benefits – would that be OK?"

    c. "Oh, by the way for just $10 more per employee per month you can add a short term disability income benefit which can help lower employee pressure for increased wages. Does that sound like something that you would like to proceed with?"

You can use this technique to add any product or service to your offering. The technique works even better if you happen to sell any individual major medical insurance. By asking the "Oh, by the way" question after each completing the application you will find that approximately 50% or more of your new clients will add a second product.

The beauty of this technique is in its simplicity. If you try to discuss the second product during the presentation of your proposal you risk clouding the issue and having the entire proposal ignored. If you try to build value for a new product during the initial fact finding meeting you risk hearing: "Right now we only want to focus on the group health." By adding an "Oh, by the way" after the decision has been made to move forward with you as the agent of choice, you make it a very simple decision for the prospect. Because the prospect is so relieved to have dealt with and resolved the group health plan the add-on will not take much thought, particularly if you are asking about a voluntary benefit. But even adding a low cost, employer-paid benefit such as a core long term disability plan of $500 monthly (generally less than $20 per employee per month) becomes less of a decision.

From the perspective of you, the benefit professional, the real beauty of this technique is that you do not have to provide a spreadsheet of choices nor get bogged down in the minutia of the product details. By choosing you as the agent of choice the prospect is placing his trust in you. He assumes that you have his best interests in mind when choosing a product for his company so there is no need for a justification. One of the biggest obstacles to the add-on sale for most benefit professionals is their own need to over-educate the prospect on the product or service being offered. The truth is that prospects do not need or want to understand insurance products. What they do want is to be able to trust the judgment of the benefit professional they choose to work with.

Here is my guarantee to you: choose one or two products that you are comfortable selling and start asking the "oh, by the way" question with every new client and you will increase your per-group revenue by a minimum of fifty percent. More importantly you will be providing valuable coverage that would not otherwise be had. Right now your clients do not know that they should add disability income, long term care, group term life or other coverage to their benefit plan. If you simply ask them if they want to add it they will likely say "not right now." But if you add the coverage through the use of the "Oh, by the way" technique and they get to deliver a claim check to an insured that would not have had that coverage in the absence of your courage, you will know that this was about more than just your per-group revenue. Using this technique is about making a real difference in the lives of working Americans and the companies that they work for.

The Relationship Rule

There is no doubt in my mind that every benefit professional reading this column provides extraordinary service to his clients. There is also no doubt that every one of you possesses an abundance of benefit knowledge. But here is the single most important concept that I can impart to you today: great service is irrelevant and your knowledge, while beneficial, will not make your accounts competitor-proof. Prospects will not do business with you simply because you promise great service or because you have an abundance of benefit knowledge. Clients will not keep your competitors out simply because you provide what you believe to be great service. And when you do the annual review and ask the client how you are doing and he tells you that you are doing a great job – well, don't get excited because there is no meat on that bone.

You may win cases because you have saved the prospect money although when you live by price you die by price. You may have an array of value-added services that can get you the case, but if you want to keep your competitors out you must build a strong relationship with both the individuals involved in managing the benefits as well as the key decision-makers.

"Clients do not care how much you do for them. They care about how much you care about and appreciate them."

In one of my recent teleclasses one of the participants responded to this idea by stating that on every renewal he tells his clients that he sees them as friends and not just clients. That statement and $1.90 will get a grande coffee at Starbucks. It is highly likely that you believe that you have really great relationships with your clients, but ask yourself these questions:

1. In between renewals, do you visit with the decision-makers within your client companies at least twice per year?
2. Do you take clients to lunch without talking about their benefits?
3. Do you send the decision-makers and HR staff handwritten birthday cards?
4. Do you know the names of the children of the decision-makers in your group clients? What about the HR staff? If so, do you ask about them?
5. When was the last time that you sent the decision-makers a handwritten note thanking them for the opportunity that they have given you to be of service to their company?

If you are not doing at least three out of the five actions in this list I can guarantee that you do not have relationships that are strong enough to lock out your competitors.

Making Service Meaningful

I can say with absolute certainty that in the last two weeks you have had at least one employee of a client call your office with a problem. The problem might have been a need for a replacement ID card, a claim issue or a need to have something explained. You resolved the issue quickly and the employee was satisfied. So here is my question:

"How does the employer know what you just did?"

Every agent that I ask this question of responds in one or two ways:

"Unless the employee tells the owner (HR Director) he will not know."

"At the end of the year I provide an update of all the services that we provided."

Both responses are meaningless. Most employees will not run to their human resources department and tell them how great your service was, although if your service was miserable they would certainly run to HR. Here is an idea that accomplishes two important objectives for you. The next time that you solve an issue for an employee send a handwritten note to the president of the company that reads:

Jim,

I just wanted to take this opportunity to thank you for allowing me to be of service to your company. What made me think about this was when John Smith called my office last Monday needing a new ID Card. We got it resolved that afternoon but it occurred to me that I haven't let you know in a while how much I appreciate the chance to work with you and your company.

Thanks
Mel Schlesinger

I can guarantee that you will receive a call of appreciation for the card. With this card you have been self-promotional while acknowledging your gratitude for the business. Do this two or three time per year and you will never lose an account to an agent of record letter.

Special Occasions

One of the great things about being in the benefits business is you have ready access to the birthdays of all of the important people in each of your accounts. The truth is that in today's world very few people get a handwritten birthday card in the mail. They may get an e-card or simply an email but that has very little impact. Opening the mailbox on the other hand and receiving a real card can truly brighten a person's day. Make it a habit to send a handwritten card to the business owners and HR staff in each of your client companies and they will feel that you truly value them.

To take relationship building one step further, ask each of the key people in your accounts about their children and marital status and make note of each. Ask about wedding anniversaries and send a handwritten note acknowledging the date and your relationship will reach the competitor-proof level.

New Business and Referrals

Cultivating relationships is about much more than competitor-proofing your accounts. Relationship building can also be a tool that creates an avalanche of referrals. Great service rarely motivates a client to simply rave about you for no reason. A birthday card or an anniversary card on the other hand is unexpected which is precisely why it is so appreciated. Recipients will tell others about how different you are from your competition, about how much you seem to really care about them as individuals.

While it sounds like this will be a lot to keep track of, new technology makes this relatively pain-free. There is technology that allows you to upload these special occasions and create cards in your handwriting that will automatically go out in the mail 5 days prior to the event. Equally valuable is the ability to create thank you cards that can be sent utilizing no more effort than sending an email. Yet a handwritten card in the mail after an appointment will have a significantly bigger impact than any email thank you ever can.

Made in the USA
Charleston, SC
27 January 2011